Supervillain of the Day

SUPERVILLAIN OF THE DAY 3

INSPECTOR FLOYD

by Katie Lynn Daniels

Cover design by Jordan Miller
Interior formatting by Aubrey Hansen

Special thanks to Elizabeth Kirkwood for reading absolutely everything I sent her, however meaningless; to Jordan Miller for his brilliant cover designs; to Elsa for her meticulous editing an invaluable assistance in revising; to Aubrey Hansen for helping clueless me with formatting and never getting tired of reading these books.

Published by:
Provide Your Own – Books
PO Box 748
Tompkinsville, KY 42167
Website: Books.ProvideYourOwn.com

Print Edition, May 2013
ISBN-13: 978-0615797199 (Provide Your Own - Books)
ISBN-10: 0615797199
Library of Congress Control Number: 2013908357

For Mr. Olson
Because you included me
Even when I had no business being there

TABLE OF CONTENTS

MONDAY'S VICTIM WAS FAIR OF FACE

Sunday night was foggy but this came as a surprise to no one. It was a distinguishing feature of London that its days were foggy, and that its nights were foggy also. Therefore, it came as no surprise to anyone that Elsie Mayfield decided to walk home alone that night in spite of the fog. She worked at a dress shop that closed at four. Every night she walked home alone, and every night was foggy, so the fog of this particular night posed no immediate impediment to her homeward voyage. What did pose an impediment was the murderous man with a knife who followed her, unseen in the grey soup.

She didn't notice him at first. She was minding her step and her business and was thinking about what she would have for supper once she got home. She heard the footsteps behind her and at first thought nothing of them, but after a few blocks they were still following. She paused uncertainly and called into the fog.

"Hello?"

Her voice was swallowed by the saturated atmosphere, and she shivered. The footsteps had stopped at the sound of her voice and did not resume. Terrified, Elsie began to run. The footsteps pursued. In her panic she lost track of her destination and became lost in the maze of streets, never seeing more than a hands breadth before her face. The relentless footsteps never faltered or slowed their pursuit. She glanced over her shoulder, striving for a glimpse of the unknown foe—a fatal mistake. Her momentary lack of attention to her flight caused her to trip and fall onto the hard pavement.

Her screams were swallowed by the thick air, and cut off suddenly. Still unseen, her killer walked quietly away, leaving the bloodied knife behind him.

....

Monday morning was foggy, too. Foggy enough that old Gruscilla wouldn't have seen the body at all, had she not tripped over it on her way to work. She had the sensibility to touch nothing and call the police but then, afraid of being late, she left the scene without waiting to be questioned. Even though she'd given her name over the phone, neither the sergeant who did the preliminaries nor the inspector who was assigned to the case were ever able to find her again.

It was seven in the morning, and Detective-Sergeant Joseph Adams moved cautiously through the fog towards the scene of the crime.

He was accompanied by two constables who conversed in low tones, their mood muted by the early morning atmosphere.

"Better call back to headquarters," Sergeant Adams said, crouching down suddenly. "We've got confirmation on a body."

The man on the left nodded and moved away, speaking into his radio.

"Go ahead and tape it off," he said to the other. "We don't want anyone else traipsing through here."

The other man went back to the car for the crime scene tape and Adams bent over the body.

She was young - probably in her early twenties. She had long blond hair that spread around her in a pool of blood. Her eyes were opened wide in terror, her mouth open forever in a wordless scream. Sergeant Adams shivered in the morning air and straightened up, looking around for other clues.

A few steps away, he found a bloodied knife. He picked it up with gloved hands and slipped it into a plastic bag, putting down a marker to show where it had been found. A further search of the area turned up nothing else, not even the dead woman's handbag.

A few minutes later Inspector McCormick arrived, muttering curses under his breath. He had grown up in the Scottish Highlands and couldn't abide London's fog, complaining about it every chance he got, which was often.

"What have we got here, then?" he asked, stepping under the crime scene tape. After twenty years of living in London his brogue was scarcely noticeable. Adams straightened up to give his report.

"The victim is a young woman, no identification. Her handbag appears to be missing. Cause of death appears to be multiple stab wounds; a knife was found a few feet away from the body. There are no other footprints or evidence on the scene. The body was found in response to an anonymous tip called in this morning."

Inspector McCormick leaned over to peer at the body and nodded absently.

"If she was running, she may have dropped her bag along the way," he said. "Take the others and go look for it."

"Yes sir," Adams said, obeying with alacrity.

Alone in the fog, McCormick lit a cigar and contemplated the problem.

Ten minutes later he emerged from contemplation to wonder why he hadn't heard from any of his officers. He was just about to try contacting Adams when his thoughts were interrupted by a little old lady who leaned heavily on a walking stick.

"Oh my," she said, staring at the victim's body.

"I'm sorry, ma'am," McCormick said hastily, stepping towards her. "This is a crime scene. You can't come through here."

"Well I live down there," she said pointedly. "I need to get home."

"Yes, I know," McCormick said. "I'll just have..." He looked around, noticing again the absence of any other policemen in the area. "If you just walk over a street you can come back up around the other way. We really can't have anyone in here until we finish collecting evidence."

4

"Well," said the old lady in an opinionated tone. "Where are your patrol men?"

It was a very good question, and McCormick was unsettled to realise that he didn't have an equally good answer.

"I don't know," he said uncertainly. "I seem to remember sending them to look for the victim's purse, but they should have found it by now."

An odd look suddenly crossed the old lady's face.

"Well that's funny," she blurted out.

"What is?" McCormick asked, alerted by the tone of her voice.

"On my way here, I saw several police officers chasing a duck around," she told him. "I thought it was quite strange, and I wonder now if they're your missing patrol men."

"A duck?" McCormick repeated incredulously. "Why would any policeman in his right mind waste his time chasing after a duck?"

"Well, that's just it, officer," the woman said. "I don't think they were in their right minds."

"What do you mean?"

"They weren't acting normal," she repeated firmly. "And neither was the other young man who was with them."

"Other young man?"

"Oh..." she shook her stick impatiently. "Why don't I just show you?"

....

Jeffry Floyd, reporter for the London Star, was perched on top of a wrought iron fence. He swung his legs back and forth like a child at the circus. Sergeant Adams and two other police officers were trying, for the seventh time (Floyd had kept careful count), to capture a white duck which seemed determined to evade them. Arms outstretched, they approached each other, keeping the duck between them. At the last minute, she squawked and darted between the legs of young Constable Finnley.

Floyd sighed.

"You could come help, you know," Adams said, glaring up at him.

Floyd shrugged.

Adams muttered something unpleasant under his breath and looked around for the evasive waterfowl.

"Maybe if we corner her against the fence..." Constable Jones suggested.

The duck wandered back to a drain in the middle of the street and stood still for a moment, head cocked on one side as if wondering what her pursuers would try next. Constable Finnley made a dive at her and she rushed almost to the edge of the street.

Floyd had drawn a white chalk circle around all of them and was watching intently to see if any of them crossed it. So far they hadn't.

"This is impossible," Adams muttered.

"Yes!" Floyd shouted, as though he had finally found the answer to an insoluble problem. "It is impossible! So why don't you, all of you, just quit? Give up! Get out of there. We'll go get coffee."

"Never!" Adams snarled. "We never give up."

"I said coffee?" Floyd tried again.

The policemen ignored him.

Inspector McCormick and his elderly escort rounded the corner.

6

"You see?" she said, grasping his arm and shaking her stick. "What did I tell you? It's not normal, is it?"

Floyd jumped off the fence when he saw him, waving both arms dramatically. "Don't come any closer!" he shouted. "It's not safe!"

"What are you talking about?" McCormick demanded. "Those are my men!"

Floyd planted himself between the inspector and the other policemen. "It's not safe," he repeated.

"What do you mean: it's not safe? Who are you? What are they doing?" he peered around Floyd in frustration.

Floyd sighed. "They're trying to catch the duck," he said. "But they can't because it's an impossible task. The duck doesn't exist." He paused to catch his breath. "If you cross that line you'll be forced to try to catch the duck too."

"Why?" McCormick demanded.

"It's a dampening field," Floyd tried to explain. "It dampens the... it tries to... oh, duck take it all, I'm not a scientist. Just don't cross that circle."

"Young man," McCormick said severely. "Would you explain what's going on in plain, honest English?"

"I'll try," Floyd promised. "But promise me you won't cross that line."

"I'll promise nothing of the sort. What's your name?"

"Floyd. Jeffry Floyd. I'm a reporter for the London Star and... just stay here, okay? Don't move. I'll be right back."

He glanced over his shoulder worriedly.

"Stay," he repeated, gesturing with both hands.

"Wait!" McCormick shouted. "You can't just—"

But Floyd was already gone, running across the street and disappearing between two houses.

McCormick started towards the policeman but hesitated just outside the line.

"Sergeant?" he asked cautiously.

"Not now, Inspector," Adams said wearily.

"What's wrong with you, Adams?" McCormick snapped.

"I've just got to finish this," Adams said, mopping his brow. "It won't take but a moment, sir."

"Snap out of it right now," McCormick ordered. "We've got a murder case to investigate."

"Yes sir," Adams said. "I know, sir. Just a moment, sir."

"What did I tell you, sir?" the old lady repeated. "Not in their right minds at all."

Before McCormick could reply, his universe was interrupted by a loud noise, accompanied by a blast of unknown origins.

The ground seemed to lurch from under him, but this was merely a perception caused by the action of falling. When everyone sat sat up, blinking through a strange purple smoke, there was no sign of the duck, the drain, or any sort of damage from the explosion.

"Everyone all right?" Floyd asked cheerfully, rejoining them. He crossed into the circle without fear and pulled Adams to his feet. "Your superior is looking for you," he added as an afterthought.

"Sergeant!" McCormick said angrily, sitting up. "What is going on? Who is this man?"

"The name is Floyd," Floyd said, sticking out his hand. "I'm a journalist for the London Star."

Inspector McCormick made a noise of derision and declined the handshake. "What just happened?" he repeated.

Constable Finnley sat up and looked around, as though waking from a bad dream. "What happened to the duck?" he asked finally.

"It vanished," Jones said, standing up. "What was that thing?"

"I don't know," Floyd admitted. "Psychic projection of some kind. An exercise in futility."

"What caused it?" Adams asked.

"Would someone tell me what is going on?" McCormick roared.

"All right!" Floyd said in surprise. "Patience! It was a dampening field of some kind. It pulled out your subconscious doubts and projected them into feelings of futility and pointlessness. You had to accomplish some impossible and utterly useless task, until eventually you got to feeling so down about it that you just gave up on life."

"But we didn't," Adams said uncertainly.

"No," Floyd smiled. "You're the British police. Of course you didn't."

"And what would cause this dampening thingy?" McCormick asked.

"Supervillains," Floyd said instantly. "Who else?"

McCormick decided not to answer that question.

"Well," Floyd said, dusting himself off. "It was nice meeting you gentlemen, but I understand you have something important to get back to and I need to go investigate this."

"Investigate?" McCormick repeated. "I thought you were a reporter."

"I am," Floyd said with wounded dignity. "And I investigate implausible phenomena such as this. So if you'll excuse me, I'd like to get back to work."

Without waiting for an answer he stalked away into the mist.

The policemen stared after him.

"He's crazy," Constable Jones declared.

"And so are all of you," McCormick said, frowning. "Chasing that duck around like it was the most important thing in the world."

Adams froze. "Duck?"

"Don't you remember? That's what you were doing—you and the constables. Chasing a duck."

Adams' mouth hung open in speechless mortification.

McCormick laughed heartily. "Now that it's all over," he said, "I'm remembering how ridiculous you all looked."

Adams dared not voice his actual thoughts and so remained silent.

"I'll forgive you," McCormick said finally, "On one condition. Tell me you found the victim's purse?"

"The victim's purse," Adams said with a start. "We did, actually. Right before..."

He trailed off in embarrassment.

"Never mind that," McCormick said. "Where is it now?"

"Finnley had it," Adams said. "Finnley!"

Constable Finnley came over at once, holding out the purse. It was made of teal-coloured faux leather and bulged, as women's purses often did. Adams took it and handed it to McCormick, who quickly went through the contents and extracted a wallet.

"Name, address, it's all here," he said. "Thank you, fellows. You've done a great job. Now get back to that crime scene before anyone else trips over it!"

The policemen were only too glad to obey.

Inspector Floyd

TUESDAY'S VICTIM WAS FULL OF GRACE

The lights came up in the great auditorium and the sole audience member came towards the front of the stage, clapping.

"Bravo!" he told the cast. "Bravo. That's all for tonight. See you at the opening night tomorrow."

The ballerinas tripped off stage, talking together, eager to get out of costume and make-up and go home for the night.

"Alexis," the director said, conversationally. One of the lead chorus members stopped and glanced back at him. He gestured her over with a head nod.

"I wish you would take an escort home tonight," he said in a low voice. "It's getting to be quite dangerous to be abroad in London at night, and we can't afford to have anything happen to you."

"You can't afford to have anything happen to anyone," she teased. "Why worry so much about me?"

She had a young, open face with teasing brown eyes. The director's eyes filled with fondness and he tweaked her chin.

"Because you're my daughter," he said, "And I care about you. You know that."

Alexis grinned, but pulled away. "Don't," she said. "You should know better than to show any sort of favouritism to me. You could get me thrown out of the company!"

"It's my company," her father said with a smile.

"Yes, I know, but," she glanced around anxiously. "No one else knows I'm related to you and I'd rather keep it that way."

Her father sighed. "Just be careful," he begged. "Please."

"I'll be fine, Daddy," she said confidently, and followed everyone else off stage.

It was an unusually warm night. The streets were well lit and busy with people coming and going, despite the late hour. Alexis set out for home in sweat pants and a t-shirt, carrying her dance gear in a bag over her shoulder. She'd left her hair pinned up in a tight bun, planning to take it down once she got home, before she showered.

She didn't take an escort, despite her father's request, and when she got off the bus at her home station she found herself quite alone. The streets here were not nearly so well illuminated as they had been in the city, and she felt suddenly afraid. What sort of monsters were lurking in the shadows that she couldn't see?

Frightened, she started to run.

....

"Another murder?" Inspector McCormick said, stepping under the yellow crime scene tape. "I've barely started on the last one! Oh, hello again, Adams."

Adams nodded, preoccupied with the form he was filling out. A hysterical school girl was giving him information at an unintelligible pace. Her mother stood behind her, soothing the girl while simultaneous ranting against the failure of the police force to protect honest people from these sorts of crimes.

The coroner had already arrived and was expecting Adams to keep up with his constant stream of information and take notes to refer to later. Two other policemen directed traffic and dealt with the growing crowd of onlookers. It was eight AM on a business morning and the stream of people going to work and school was continuous.

"Got an ID on her yet?" McCormick asked.

"Yes sir," Adams said, searching through the stack of forms for a completed one. "Stage name: Alexis Duvarre. Real name: Alexis Jones."

"Stage name?"

"She's an up and coming ballerina," Adams explained, handing him the form.

"Is it a supervillain?" the schoolgirl was saying, brushing away tears. "Or is it some kind of killer? I lived just down the street from her. Are they coming after me next?"

"My daughter deserves some guarantee of her safety!" the mother said angrily.

"Ma'am, I assure you, nothing is going to happen to you or your daughter. The police will be doing everything they can to look into this matter. Now if you could just tell me your names and address? We may need to contact you later."

"If it's a supervillain something has to be done," the mother said.

"Same cause of death as the other?" McCormick asked.

"I don't know about the other," the coroner said, "It was multiple stab wounds that killed her."

"We'll do everything we can," Adams promised the mother.

"Did you find the murder weapon?" McCormick asked.

"Hey, what's going on?" a burly middle-aged man asked, coming over. "A murder, eh?"

"The knife was left by the body," Adams said, gesturing distractedly.

"I'm sorry, you can't be in here," one of the constables said ineffectively.

"I could use some backup down here," Adams spoke into his radio.

"Are you listening to me?" the mother screeched.

"Any family?" McCormick asked, sidling over to look at the knife.

"Her father owns the ballet company she danced for," Adams said. "Arthur Jones. He's been contacted and is on his way down now."

"Is there anything I can help you folks with?" the civilian intruder asked.

"Yes," the patrolman shouted, losing patience. "Go about your day and let us work in peace."

"Thank you for your time," Adams told the witness. "We'll be in touch. Thank you."

"But is it safe?" the mother asked. "What about the killer?"

"We'll catch him," Adams promised.

"I heard this wasn't the first murder of this sort," the civilian intruder said conversationally. "Ya'll dealing with a serial killer of some kind?"

"A serial killer?" the mother screamed.

The daughter burst into tears again.

"Please," Adams begged. "Take your daughter home. Everything will be fine; I promise you. We're doing everything we can."

"And what if that's not enough?"

"What's the time of death?" McCormick asked, wondering why everyone seemed so distracted.

"About one in the morning, sir," said the Coroner.

"Please," Adams said. "Just take your daughter and go home. There's nothing to worry about."

"Please sir," the constable said. "You can't be in here. Just go about your day."

"I expect protection," the mother said, finally leaving, one arm firmly around her daughter. "I expect the police to do their job."

"Yes ma'am, of course," Adams said desperately. "We'll be in touch. Thank you."

"Could they be connected, d'ya think?" McCormick mused aloud. "There's no connection between the victims yet, but the method of death and the timing seems suspicious."

"We're still checking contacts on the woman who died yesterday," Adams said. "This girl's dad is on his way down here."

17

"What do you think, Sergeant?" McCormick asked. "Could they be connected?"

Adams shrugged. "It seems hard to tell one way or the other at this point," he said wearily. "I got the names and addresses of everyone who claims to have known her so far," he added, handing over another list. "Just in case you want to question them later."

"Alexis?" a panicked voice broke into the chaos. "Alexis!"

"Sir," Adams said, trying to forestall him, "sir!"

"Let me see my daughter!" the man said. "I insist on seeing my daughter!"

"Mr. Jones?" Inspector McCormick said, coming forward.

"Let me see my daughter," the director said angrily.

The coroner shrugged and stepped back, out of his line of sight.

The fight went instantly out of the bereaved father and he sagged forward.

"Alexis," he whispered brokenly, taking a step towards her.

"I'm sorry," Adams said instinctively.

"What happened?" Jones demanded. "I told her to watch out for supervillains, I told her to take an escort... Alexis..."

He knelt beside her, his voice breaking with emotion. The policemen stood around, subdued. The crowd of spectators quieted, finally realising this wasn't any of their business.

"Did Alexis have any enemies?" McCormick asked gently. "Anyone who would want to harm her?"

Jones shook his head. "No one," he said. "She was just a troupe member, not even a threat to the leads."

"Do you know where she was last night?"

"At the theatre... rehearsing. She left a little after midnight to come straight home. She only lives a block from here. Oh, Alexis..."

He sobbed and hid his face in his hands. McCormick glanced at Adams.

"I'll need your address and phone number," Adams said, "So we can get in touch with you later."

Mr. Jones nodded his head. "Can I... can I take the body?" he asked hesitantly.

"I'm afraid we'll have to keep it a while longer," the sergeant said regretfully. "We'll be in touch."

Jones wept openly as the coroner gestured to his assistant and they took the girl's body away on a stretcher, loading it into a waiting van.

Adams beckoned one of his constables over.

"This is Constable Smith," he explained. "He'll take you home."

Jones nodded and let himself be led away.

Realising the show was over, the crowd began to quiet and drift away.

"So we have two murders, seemingly unconnected, but with certain similarities," McCormick said thoughtfully. "Let's hope to God that there's not a third."

....

In a part of town long ago overrun by those of the super- and sub-human variety, where no sane person dared to venture, on a street lined by dirty

19

buildings and ominously darkened windows, there was a club which had a poor reputation even before the appearance of supervillains six months earlier. It now served as one of the many haunts of henchmen—those who had superpowers but weren't capable enough to be able to utilise them to their full ability. Instead, henchmen worked for supervillains who came up with the evil schemes they all longed to fulfil. When off-duty or unemployed, this was where they came to fight, squabble, complain, and indulge in human vices.

It was also where Floyd came for information, or when he was simply bored.

Raucous laughter could be heard even out on the street. The crowd of henchmen inside had cleared an open space in the middle of the floor where two opponents were fighting to the death. Floyd staggered and fell, and a hiss went up from the crowd. Floyd sat up cautiously, then grinned at the spectators.

His opponent took a step backwards, but no one saw him. In fact, no one saw him at all. He was invisible.

Floyd stood, closed his eyes, and waited.

For several moments nothing happened.

The spectators held their breath.

Floyd stood completely motionless, looking at nothing, and barely even breathing.

There was a subtle breath of wind and Floyd moved. Faster then the eye could follow he reached out and grabbed nothing. He jerked, kicked, spun around and hit, and there was a disembodied scream of pain. Then nothing.

Floyd turned to the crowd and bowed in triumph. The henchmen applauded and cheered appropriately.

"Now then," Floyd said, going over to the bar and scooping up his share of the bets that had been placed. There was a muted groan of protest. Floyd never lost a match, but there were always those who hoped, or newbies who didn't know better.

"Who's ready to start talking?" Floyd asked, glancing around the room.

There was a shuffling of feet, and everyone found something else to occupy their attention.

"Come on," Floyd said coaxingly. "Don't make me kill one of you."

No one answered.

"What about you?" Floyd said, singling out a skinny green fellow. "What do you know?"

Everyone took an instinctive step away, leaving Floyd's choice isolated.

"What do you want to know?" the unfortunate stammered.

"Dampening fields," Floyd said. "Who's making them?"

"I-I..."

"Tell me!" Floyd snapped.

"I don't know!" the skinny green thing shrieked, and disappeared under a table.

"Okay..." Floyd said slowly, looking around for another victim. "Who does know?"

No answer. Floyd returned to the invisible man and rummaged his pockets. He drew his hand back holding a shiny silver gun. A murmur of fear ran around the room.

"Dampening fields," Floyd repeated tersely.

"It was Doctor Clockwork!" someone shouted. Floyd turned, but not quickly enough to see who the informant was.

"Doctor Clockwork," he repeated. "That's a start. Where is he now?"

Hesitance.

"Where?"

"He's dead," a burly man at one of the tables said flatly. "Somethin' took him out two nights ago. Figgered it was you, actually."

"No," Floyd said slowly, "it wasn't. So who did it? Another villain? Some petty squabble? Come on! Someone has to know!"

Everyone looked around and didn't answer.

Floyd rolled his eyes.

"We don't know," an elastic squeak chirped up. "That's just it. We don't know."

"Professor Nobody was killed yesterday," a frog-like creature put in. "Stabbed through the heart. No reason at all. No one saw him do it."

The undercurrent of fear was tangible.

Floyd took the money out of his pocket and put it back on the bar.

"Anyone who can tell me who killed either Professor Nobody or Doctor Clockwork can have it," he said. "Just speak up and stop protecting your employer!"

The room quivered. Everyone wanted the money. No one said anything.

Floyd sighed and stood up. "If anything should jog your memory," he said, putting both money and gun away, "you can leave a message for me here. And listen: if someone else is taking out the supervillains, I will find out."

He looked around, his face a warning and his eyes a promise. The henchmen relaxed and nodded.

"Thanks for the sport, guys," Floyd said, letting himself out. "See you tomorrow."

A small hand reached out and grabbed his coat as he walked past. Startled he turned.

The still-innocent face of Stabby looked up at him. The child-henchman clutched a plastic dragon tightly in one hand and stared at Floyd with wide-eyed fear.

"Are we in danger?" he asked.

No one else in the room would dare to ask the question, but they all wanted to know the answer.

"I don't know," Floyd said honestly, pulling away from the kid. "If I find out... I'll tell you."

....

Forever after, Floyd would swear that he was only passing through, minding his own business, and that the fact that his path led past Adams' crime scene was the merest coincidence.

And just as vehemently, Sergeant Adams would insist that Floyd was a meddler, that he would always be a meddler, and that the only reason for his presence in a quiet suburban area was for meddling.

It was nearly noon and the crime scene was still crawling with reporters, bystanders, and various experts.

"Can't you do something about all these people?" Inspector McCormick growled.

Adams, who wished very much that something could be done about them, promised to do his best and tried once again—shouting at the crowd to be about their business.

"What's going on?" said a far too familiar voice, and a head poked its way around Adams with no more respect for the policeman's orders then he had for personal space. "Oh, hello again," he added, catching sight of Inspector McCormick, and ignoring the bloodstains the good inspector was inspecting.

"Floyd..." Adams said warningly.

"Oh, it's you," the Inspector grunted, sitting back on his heels. "The duck guy. Have you found any more of those... what did you call 'em? Disrupter fields?"

"Dampening fields," Floyd corrected. "Let's put it this way. If you see a drain where there shouldn't be one, don't go near it. Or send someone else in first. Ditto for ducks."

"I'll bear that in mind," McCormick said. "What brings you around here, anyway?" he added, peering up at him. "Sort of an out-of-the-way place for supervillains, isn't it?"

Floyd shrugged. "I'm a reporter," he said. "I smelled a news story."

Adams closed his eyes for a moment, trying to ward off the headache he sensed approaching.

"Thought you specialised in the paranormal and supernatural," McCormick pointed out.

"Unexplained phenomena," Floyd corrected. "But you're right—I just happened to be passing through. It's a sort of short-cut to my destination."

"I see," McCormick frowned in suspicion. "And where might your destination be?"

Floyd grinned. "Can't give away all my secrets, now can I, Inspector?"

"I'll be keeping an eye on you," McCormick said, shaking a warning finger in his direction. "A very close eye indeed."

Floyd sidled away. "The sergeant already does a job of that," he said. "Constantly keeping tabs on me, he is."

Adams glared.

"Well," Floyd ducked back to the civilian side of the crime scene tape. "I'll be seeing you around!"

And with a cheerful wave, he scampered off.

"Hmmm," McCormick said, watching him go.

"Indeed," Adams agreed whole-heartedly.

"How well do you know him?" McCormick asked thoughtfully.

"Floyd?" Adams repeated, startled. "Not well. Just enough to keep a close eye on him, I suppose."

"Hmm," McCormick said. "He works for the London Star?"

"That's right."

"Wouldn't put anything past him, then."

"Not really," Adams ruefully concurred.

....

When Adams returned home late Tuesday night, he opened his front door to the sound of his telephone ringing. He was not accustomed to answering the telephone when at home. This was partly because he was so rarely at home that he wasn't usually around to answer when telemarketers called, and no one else had his number, except for family members he never heard from.

Well, hardly ever.

"Hello, Joey," said a teasing, feminine voice on the other side of the line. "This is Kate! How have you been... big brother?"

Adams realised that his day could not possibly get any stranger.

WEDNESDAY'S MURDERS ARE FULL OF WOE

Morning was a grey and bitter affair, with the after-taste of something supposed to be tasteless. The sky was the colour of smog, the air was the colour of smog, the buildings, streets, and river were all the colour of smog, and the faint, acrid smell of smoke seemed to linger much in the manner of an imagined slight.

It was hard to make out the shape of a person in a long, grey coat blending into its surroundings. The policeman on duty had to blink several times to convince himself it was really there, and when he did he shouted at it to halt.

The shapeless form paused, turned, and there was nothing grey or languid about the pale, bloodied body he carried in his arms.

The policeman froze in unease, and his hand tightened around his baton.

"It's all right," the figure said, coming towards the policeman. "He had a bad fall. I'm taking him home."

"He's dead," the policeman said sternly. "You're not going anywhere."

The stranger glanced anxiously over his shoulder, and then down at the body in his arms.

"Who are you going to call?" he asked, somewhat worried.

"None of your business," the policeman snapped. "Set the body down, slowly now."

To his surprise the stranger obeyed, kneeling cautiously with his burden.

The policeman got out his handcuffs. "Put your hands on your head," he ordered.

The stranger did so, and the officer cuffed the criminal, daring to hope he would come out of this alive. He stood a safe distance away while calling back to headquarters, never taking his eyes off of his prey. He needn't have worried. The stranger never budged.

"All right then," the constable said, coming over. "Someone is on their way down."

"Who?" the stranger enquired, seemingly calm.

"None of your business," the policeman snapped. "What's your name?"

"Floyd. Jeffry Floyd. Please, I'd like to make a phone call."

"To who?"

"Sergeant Adams of Scotland Yard."

The constable paused, squinting at him in puzzlement. "You're with the police?" he asked dubiously.

"No." Floyd shook his head. "The sergeant is a friend of mine. He can get me out of this."

"Is that a fact?" said the constable, and put in another call.

Then they waited in frosty silence that rivalled the morning air for unpleasantness, each caught up in fear and trepidation.

The policeman worried that his captive would turn psychotic, and murder him in his escape, and Floyd wondered if Adams would be able to get him out of this scrape or if he was better off running now, destined to be a fugitive forever.

Neither man budged.

Finally the stalemate was broken by the wail of a siren, and a squad car pulled up, spewing out Inspector McCormick and Sergeant Adams.

Sergeant Joseph Adams had gone to bed secure in the knowledge that his day couldn't get any stranger. He'd forgotten about the rest of the week.

He had also forgotten about Floyd's capacity for getting into trouble. His attitude upon reaching the crime scene was one of long-suffering patience.

Floyd looked up at him in hope, still on his knees on the pavement.

"Sir?" the constable said eagerly. "Thank you for coming."

"What have we got here?" McCormick asked gruffly.

"Thanks for calling," Adams said. "You did the right thing. You can get up now, Floyd."

"He was coming out of that building," the constable explained rapidly. "Carrying the body."

"You've got a lot of explaining to do, young man," McCormick said. "Can you explain your actions here?"

Floyd stood up and held out his hands.

"Take the cuffs off of him," Adams instructed.

"Leave them," McCormick countered. The constable glanced from one to the other questioningly. McCormick moved to inspect the body.

"He's a henchman," Floyd volunteered. "Name of Stabby."

"Stop making up fairy tales!" the inspector roared. "This kid was no more a supervillain than you or I."

"Unless he is a supervillain," the constable said helpfully.

"I didn't say he was a supervillain," Floyd protested. "I said he was a henchman. There's a difference. The kid was psychic; he saw things before they happened and sold that information to the highest bidder."

"He's telling the truth, incidentally," Adams interjected. "I've never known Floyd to be wrong about a supervillain."

"Is that so?" the inspector growled. "Young man, do you know that you're under suspicion on three murder counts?"

Floyd's jaw dropped and he stared wordlessly.

"The best thing you can do right now is to make a full confession," the inspector said. "Tell me how you did it."

"But I didn't!" Floyd stammered. "I didn't kill anyone! I don't even know what you... three? Who's been murdered? What has it got to do with me?"

"You were found with the body of the third."

30

"Stabby?" Floyd repeated in growing confusion. "But I didn't kill him. I don't know who did, but I'm trying to find out."

"You're trying to find out?" the inspector scoffed.

"Stabby was a henchman," Floyd said, trying to be cooperative.

"Mm," said the inspector noncommittally.

"Tell him," Floyd said to Adams desperately. "Tell them I didn't do it. I didn't murder anyone, Joseph. You know I didn't. I couldn't possibly! Why would I hurt innocent people? Why would anyone think I would?"

"Because you were found with the body of one?" Adams suggested, raising his eyebrows.

"He was a henchman," Floyd repeated.

"He was a seven-year-old little boy," Adams argued.

"So?"

"So, henchmen are evil!"

"So are little kids," Floyd argued. "Superhuman or not. Don't you remember being one?"

Without warning Adams' thoughts jumped to a phone call he'd had the night before, and he didn't answer.

"Listen," Floyd said earnestly. "Stabby was a henchman. New guy. Smart. Psychic. He'd see things before they happened and sell the information to the highest bidder. I didn't kill him—I wouldn't have! He sold information to me, too. No one would have; he's far more valuable alive then dead. I can't think of any reason to kill him; he's still just a kid no matter how much of a pain he might be. I just talked to him last night. I was going down to see him this morning, actually, when I found the body. Well, I followed some rats there. Not actual rats, it's a word for... never mind. I was going to take him back to—never mind that either, you really don't want to know—when a policeman stopped me. I could have got away but I knew you would never forgive me if you found out."

"Stop," Adams said, rubbing his forehead. "You buy information from henchmen?"

"All the time," Floyd said promptly. "They don't have any loyalty, you know. Being evil and all."

"All right, back to the murders," Adams said. "This kid, Stabby, he was murdered by the same person we've been investigating."

"Who's that?" Floyd asked promptly.

"If we knew that it wouldn't be an investigation," Adams explained.

"Tell me about the other murders," Floyd said.

"I don't know that I'm authorised to do that," Adams said cautiously.

"So explain to the good inspector that I'm not a killer and get him to explain," Floyd said.

"It's not that easy," Adams sighed.

"Why not?"

"You were found with the body," Adams repeated, as though that explained everything.

"So?" Floyd repeated. "That doesn't mean I did it!"

McCormick lost patience. "How did you meet this clown?" he asked.

"Remember the incident back in January?" Adams interjected. "That's how we met."

"You were involved with that?"

"Yes sir."

"And you didn't file a report?"

Adams shrugged. "What would I have said?"

"Good point," McCormick mused. "Good point."

"Someone's killing the supervillains," Floyd blurted out. "You know those dampening fields you asked me about? I haven't been able to disarm them all because their creator is dead, and he's the only one with a map showing all the locations! Nobody knows why he's dead, and it has them scared. Anything that has villains scared is pretty dangerous. Now you're investigating murders, too. I think we're looking for the same killer. Stabby was the first body I found, but you said he was killed by your murderer, so what can you tell me about the others?"

McCormick was taken off guard by this sudden analysis.

"You're still suspected of murder," he stammered.

"No, I'm not," Floyd said quickly. "Because your first priority is to stop a murderer and you're never going to do that without me."

"Why not?" McCormick demanded.

"Because the murderer is a supervillain," Floyd explained. "And you have no idea how to deal with that."

"And you do?" McCormick sneered.

"I do," Floyd said confidently. "And if you'll get these cuffs off of me and show me your case files I'll prove it to you."

"I thought you were just a reporter?"

"Since when is a man not allowed to have more than one interest?" Floyd demanded. "I've been fascinated with supervillains since the outbreak began. I have studied them and learned everything I can. I'm an expert when it comes to defeating them. You need my help."

McCormick dithered for a minute. "All right," he said finally. "All right. But you had better crack this case, young man. If you don't catch this murderer, and prove it conclusively, I'll have you arrested, I swear it."

"That won't happen," Floyd said fervently. "You won't regret this, Inspector."

"Don't believe him," Adams said mournfully. "You'll regret it every time you see his face."

Floyd grinned eagerly. "Can you take these cuffs off now?" he asked. "We've got ourselves a murderer to catch."

....

The inspector took them both back to his office and handed Floyd a sheaf of papers.

"The first murder victim was Elsie Mayfield," he explained. "She was 29 and worked as a dress clerk. The second murder was Alexis Jones; she was a ballerina. 21 years old. The third victim is Alan Bradshaw, age 7. All the victims were stabbed multiple times in the chest. In all three cases the murder weapons was found on the scene. No fingerprints were recovered. Other than all being blades the weapons do not resemble the others in the slightest."

Floyd looked through the pictures and tossed them aside. "These people weren't murdered by a supervillain," he said. "Whoever did this was very much human."

"What?" McCormick gaped. "You said..."

"I was guessing," Floyd interrupted. "I'm not saying a supervillain isn't behind it somehow. In fact, I'm not saying anything. None of it makes sense."

"Explain why you think it couldn't have been a supervillain," Adams interjected.

"I don't think," Floyd snapped. "I know. It's all in the force of the blow. If the killer had superpowers the knife would have gone clean through."

"So what about a villain with some other kind of power?" McCormick asked. "Freezing his victim or... or appearing as an illusion or something?"

"It wasn't a villain," Floyd repeated, shaking his head. "There's no anger or violence in these killings."

"Killings are the definition of anger and violence!" Adams argued.

"Yes," Floyd agreed. "But these bodies are intact, left in the street, with the knife still in them. This is a human crime."

McCormick scratched his head. "Walk me through it," he said.

Floyd sighed. "Okay," he said. "Villains are driven by hate, anger, greed, etc."

"So are people," Adams pointed out.

"Right," Floyd said, irritated, "But in villains these traits are amplified. So while a human might kill someone in a bout of anger, that's not enough for an angry villain. He's not going to kill—he's going to tear the body apart limb from limb."

"So maybe the villain wasn't angry?" Adams suggested.

Floyd shook his head. "You don't understand," he said. "Villains don't commit murders. Massacres, yes. They take prisoners, they torture them to death. They take hostages to prove a point, but they don't skulk around in the dead of the night killing random strangers. It's not their style. They're as proud as they are evil and they want everyone to know what they're doing and why they're doing it."

He stood up and brushed his hands together. "This man was killed by an ordinary human being like you or me. Well, not like me," he amended, "like you or Sergeant Adams here."

"So we're looking for a human killer?" McCormick clarified.

Floyd sighed and looked through the pictures again.

"No," he said, shaking his head. "You're looking for at least three."

"Three what?" Adams demanded.

"They're all different killers," Floyd said. "The deaths look the same, but they're not really. The victims and locations are completely random. The method is the same, but not identical. They're all knifings, yes, but each time the blow is in a different location, the blades are all different types. There's no connection in why the victims were chosen."

"So we have a murderer and two copycats?" McCormick suggested.

"No," Floyd repeated. "I think you have a gang and a mastermind."

"A gang and a what?"

Floyd sighed. "Most supervillains operate alone," he explained. "The only time they work together is if one is in direct control of the others, through hypnotism or drugs or something. The leader of such a group is called a mastermind. In theory a mastermind could control ordinary humans as well, or instead of, supervillains."

"And is that what you think is going on here?" Adams asked.

"I don't know," Floyd said, rubbing his forehead. "The entire problem is giving me a headache. I need more information and no one is talking. I can double check my database, but I don't know of anyone who could do this..."

"Database?" McCormick queried.

"Oh," Floyd said scribbling down a web address for him. "I keep a database of all known supervillains and henchmen. Check it out. It might come in handy sometime."

He handed over the card. "Now," he said brightly, "If you officers are done treating me like a common criminal, I'm going to get back to work."

"Wait, Floyd," Adams said, following him out of the office. "I'm not going to be able to make our meeting tomorrow."

Floyd froze. "What?" he repeated.

"My sister is coming to London," Adams explained. "Since I haven't seen her in six months I thought I would spend some time with her, instead of you."

Floyd's face retained it's expression of stupefied amazement.

"You have a sister?"

"Call me sometime tomorrow evening, all right?" Adams said, ignoring the question. "And if anything important comes up you let Inspector McCormick know right away."

"But—" Floyd stammered.

"Great," Adams said, slapping him on the back. "Have a nice day."

And he disappeared into the bowels of Scotland Yard, leaving Floyd staring around like the bottom of his world had fallen out.

THURSDAY'S VILLAINS HAVE FAR TO GO

Kate Adams was as unlike her brother as any sibling could be. Her hair was a dark auburn, and quite long when she let it down, which she never did. She was as small and slight as he was tall and strong, but the curious green eyes that peered out at the world were the same.

She smiled brightly when she stepped out of the train station, searching the crowd for a familiar face.

"Joseph!" she squealed, running the few short steps to hug him.

"Hello, Kate," he said, calmly, as usual, returning the hug.

"I'm so glad you could make it," she said. "I hope I didn't upset your plans too terribly."

"I made it work," Adams assured her. "What brings you to London?"

"Oh, it's a business trip," she said, carefully sparing the details. "I'm only here through Saturday."

"Couldn't you lengthen your stay?" Adams asked pleadingly.

She smiled winningly. "Maybe," she teased. "We'll see how things go tomorrow."

"How was your trip?"

"Uneventful," she said. "I hear you have quite a supervillain problem here."

"Well, we keep it under control," Adams said noncommittally.

"Under control?" Kate repeated. "How do you control villains?"

"We manage," Adams said, trying to backpedal. "How about Cardiff?"

"Quiet," Kate said. "Hardly a problem at all."

"Fascinating," Adams said, holding open the door for her.

"Oh," the waitress said in surprise. "You're with someone different today!"

"This is my sister," Adams introduced her.

"What happened to that odd young man you always have?" the waitress asked curiously. Kate raised her eyebrows.

"He'll be here next week," Adams promised with a grin.

"She seemed to know you," Kate observed.

"I come here pretty often," Adams explained.

"This 'odd young man' was the date you had to cancel?" Kate asked coyly.

"He's a friend," Adams said shortly. "We meet every week."

"I didn't mean to interrupt such an established event," Kate apologized.

"It's fine," Adams assured her. "He'll survive."

"If you say so," Kate smiled.

"I do," Adams said, ending the subject. "So tell me about your life. Are you still dating Bryan?"

"Sometimes," Kate shrugged.

"How do you only date someone 'sometimes'?" her brother demanded.

"Well, let's see," she pretended to think. "When he asks me if I want to go out sometimes I say yes, and sometimes I say no."

"And he puts up with that?"

Kate grinned. "Sometimes," she replied enigmatically. "So what's new in your life?"

Joseph shrugged. "We're tracking down a serial killer," he said. "Only, according to Floyd, it's not a serial killer, it's multiple killers. Not sure I buy the theory or not."

"Floyd?" Kate's ears perked. "That's quite a name."

"He's quite a character," Joseph said dryly.

"I'd like to meet him," Kate said.

"No, you wouldn't," Joseph said fervently.

Kate laughed. "Why not?" she asked.

"Well," Joseph hesitated. "Floyd is..."

He was interrupted by the tinkle of the doorbell, and the man himself walked in, carrying a frightening looking assault rifle.

"Everyone on the floor!" he shouted.

Adams stood up and put his sister behind him.

"That includes you, Joseph," Floyd said pointedly.

"He seems to know you," Kate said anxiously, peering over her brother's shoulder.

"Yes, he does," Adams agreed.

"Everyone do what he says," he said in a calm voice, and the sight of the uniform made everyone obey.

"Aren't you going to stop him?" Kate asked, crouching under the table next to her brother.

"He's not the supervillain," Adams assured her.

"Then who is?" Kate demanded.

"Come out!" Floyd shouted, and the safety came off with a sharp click.

People screamed and glass shattered as he opened fire.

Huddled under the tables, no one was harmed. Floyd stood in the center of the room, waiting.

"That's the villain," Adams said, pointing.

Slowly, unbelievably, all the glass began to come together. From every corner of the restaurant, it rushed together, drawn by some invisible force. It formed into a towering pile directly in front of Floyd, and resolved itself into a shape with a head, a body, two arms and two legs. The head resettled itself until it had eyes, a nose, and a mouth.

The mouth smiled, and then hissed. The bits of broken glass rattled together.

Kate watched through the chair and table legs with undisguised fascination.

Floyd pointed the gun at the glassman and grinned manically.

"Now you start talking," he threatened, "Or I start shooting again."

The glass rattled together, but no words came out.

"Start talking!" Floyd shouted.

"What..." The words came slowly, almost painfully, like slivers of glass being pulled out of flesh. "Do... you... want... to... know?"

"Who killed Stabby?" Floyd said crisply.

The glassman shook his head.

"Who killed him?" Floyd repeated, raising the rifle. "Answer me, you lump of kinetic energy, or you'll never see a piece of glass again!"

The glassman held up both hands in protest.

"He doesn't seem dangerous," Kate whispered.

"You shouldn't watch this," Adams suggested.

Kate shook her head, her eyes glued to what she could see of the scene.

"Who killed Stabby?" Floyd repeated, carefully enunciating each word. "You know who I'm talking about—psychic kid, loved dinosaurs?"

"Don't... know..."

"Don't lie to me!" Floyd screamed.

The glassman continued to mumbled incoherently, shaking his head, and holding out his hands in innocence.

"All right," Floyd said, calming down somewhat. "Here's an easy one. Who's killing all the supervillains?"

"Don't... know..."

"Why?"

"You... asked... yesterday. If... you... find... out... tell... us."

"You tell me something useful," Floyd said, "or you won't walk out of here, I swear it."

"Don't... know..."

More screams as Floyd opened fire again. Kate shrieked and hid her face in Adam's shoulder as glass shards flew everywhere.

43

The stutter of machine gun fire went on for quite sometime, combined with the repeated shattering of glass. Finally it stopped. A few footsteps crunched, and Kate looked up.

Floyd stood surrounded by finely crushed glass, his face and hands spotted with blood where it had struck him. His face was set in grim lines and the gun hung limply from his right hand.

"Stick close to me," Adams told Kate. "I can't check to make sure you're following, so don't stay behind."

"What are you going to do?" she asked, but Adams was already moving out.

"Drop the gun!" he shouted. Floyd turned in surprise.

"Drop the gun and put your hands on your head," Adams repeated. "You're under arrest."

"You're arresting me?" Floyd repeated incredulously.

"I'm not going to tell you again," Adams snapped.

To Kate's surprise, Floyd obeyed, dropping the gun, kneeling in the glass, and putting both hands on the back of his head. Adams pulled a pair of handcuffs out of his back pocket and cuffed his wrists together.

"Oh come on," Floyd complained.

"Get moving," Adams snapped, picking up the heavy machine gun rifle.

Floyd stumbled to his feet and headed for the door. The patrons peering over the ruined tables mustered a small cheer for the victory of law and order.

Outside sirens began to sound.

"Where did you get the gun?" Adams asked.

"I have my means," Floyd said.

"Tell me," Adams hissed into his ear, "right now."

Floyd sighed. "I borrowed it from a guard over in Winchester."

Adams swore. Kate raised her eyebrows and stuck close.

The cars that were pulling up outside were not police cars. They were armored, and the men inside were armed.

"You know what?" Adams said, tugging on Floyd's handcuffs. "Change of plans. We're going out the back. Quickly."

"I don't understand," Kate said.

"Stick close," Adams warned her.

"You expect me to run in handcuffs?" Floyd asked, as they walked out the back door.

"Just do it," Adams said tersely.

"Where are we going?"

"To the station."

"You really intend to arrest me?"

"I already did."

"Joseph..."

"Just be glad I got to you first," Adams snapped. "Now go!"

They ran through narrow alleys, avoiding being seen by anyone at any cost, finally arriving back at the police station.

"Please," Floyd begged. "Don't do this to me."

"Listen to me," Adams said, pulling him around to face him. "You stole a gun from a member of the Queen's Guard. That's worse than terrorism, Floyd. That's treason."

"So?" Floyd shrugged. "You can't charge me with treason. I'm not a citizen."

"You're an idiot!" Adams shouted. "Now get moving."

"Sergeant Adams!" McCormick greeted him enthusiastically. "Good, you're here. You can come with me. Did you hear about the shooting? Do you think that's in any way connected to— Hello, Floyd."

Floyd glared. McCormick glanced from him to Adams, looking for an explanation.

"This is the shooter," Adams said. "I was there first."

"I was shooting a supervillain!" Floyd said angrily.

"Where did you get the gun?" McCormick asked.

Floyd shut up abruptly.

"He took the gun from the supervillain," Adams lied for him. "We don't know how the villain got it."

Kate opened her mouth to protest and shut it again.

McCormick understood. "I'll pass that information along," he promised. "Do you think we can dispense with the handcuffs?"

"No," Adams said bluntly. "In fact, if you don't mind, I'll go leave him in an interrogation room while we clear this up."

"Whatever you think best," McCormick said. "Just get over here and help me."

"I'll stay here," Kate said, watching Adams handcuff Floyd to a metal table. Adams hesitated, and then agreed.

"Keep an eye on him," he said, pointing for emphasis.

"Oh," he stuck his head back in the door. "Kate, this is Floyd. Floyd, this is my sister, Kate."

Floyd looked in surprise from one to the other but Adams was already gone.

"So," Kate said with a smile, perching on the edge of the table. "You're different."

Floyd opened his mouth but no words came out.

"You're pretty well acquainted with my brother," Kate said, ticking the points off on her fingers. "You seem to be acquainted with the police station as well. The inspector knew you by name. You're looking for information on the death of someone named Stabby, and you seemed to be pretty upset about it. You know how to fight supervillains, and appear to understand a great deal about them in general. You are not a citizen of Great Britain, and you had no compunctions against stealing an assault rifles from the Queen's Guard, despite the obvious consequences such an action carries. Did I miss anything?"

Floyd shook his head, still speechless.

"You're an undercover agent," Kate concluded. "With a reputation for breaking the rules, but indispensable to your superiors."

Floyd shook his head again. Kate frowned and caught his chin in her hand, staring at his face.

"Weren't you cut pretty badly by the glass?" she said, tracing his cheek with her other finger. He trembled slightly at her touch but made no answer. She wiped the specks of blood away. The skin underneath was unbroken.

"Who are you?" Kate demanded.

Floyd stared at her warily, and didn't answer.

Kate laughed and let go of him, walking around to sit in the other chair.

"I'm not going to hurt you," she said. "I'm just curious."

"You're really Joseph's sister?" Floyd blurted out.

Kate laughed again, her voice tinkling like little bells. "Yes," she said. "I am."

"Older or younger?"

"Younger."

"He never mentions you," Floyd said wonderingly. "I've worked with him for six months and never knew he had family."

"Everyone has family," Kate said pragmatically.

Floyd glanced away.

"Oh," Kate said understandingly. "I'm sorry."

"Not your fault," Floyd mumbled, shaking his head.

"So what's your story?" Kate asked. "Where are you from?"

Floyd found he had nothing to say. He went through all the truths and half-truths he knew and he couldn't bring himself to lie to her.

Kate's expression softened in sympathy and understanding and she said, "That bad, huh?"

He looked up suddenly and caught her gaze and found himself speechless.

"It's all right," Kate said. "I have secrets, too."

"I'm nothing like my brother," she said, trying to lighten the mood. "My brother," she explained, "Is OCD. He colour coded his closet. Nothing could touch the floor. It drove me nuts; we used to fight all the time. When he would play with toy cars he would line them up along a ruler. Who do you work for, Floyd?"

"I work for the London Star," he said, startled by the change in topic.

48

"You're a reporter?" she said in considerable surprise. "You write about alien sightings and transmutations and things?"

"Unexplained phenomena," Floyd said without enthusiasm. "Yeah."

"Do you actually believe in that kind of thing?"

"Nope," Floyd said shortly.

"So why do you write it?"

"It's a job," Floyd said, stating the obvious.

"Yes, I know," Kate laughed. "But why don't you get another one?"

Floyd hesitated. "I don't actually write that well," he tried to explain.

"You can learn."

But I don't have a birth certificate, Floyd thought desperately. *And I don't have a visa. And what can I say that won't make me sound like a loser?*

"I don't really care much about writing," he blurted out. "I'd much rather put my energies into trying to stop the supervillains."

"Oh, supervillains!" Kate said delightedly. "I was wondering when we would come back to that. You're a reporter who is a supervillain expert, who can handle a machine gun, and who is apparently impervious to injury.

"Tell me," Kate said, running her fingers over the polished metal table distractedly. "What do you think of the superhero initiative?"

"It's a stupid idea," Floyd said vehemently. "Everyone knows that attempting to create superheroes never works. The more they try to fix the problem the worse they make it. Fight supervillains, by all means, but do it by ordinary human methods. Build containment fields, or large projectile weapons or underground bunkers, but don't put your money into anything as idiotic and as likely to backfire as superheroes."

"You feel very strongly on this subject," Kate observed.

"Like I said, I think it's something we should all be involved in."

"I think we don't know anything for certain," Kate countered. "And that it's always better to reach out and explore and take the risk then to hide in bunkers waiting for the inevitable."

"There are plenty of ways to reach out and explore without meddling in the impossible," Floyd said. "Build rocket ships or work on interstellar communication or something."

"Interstellar communication?" Kate laughed. "That's less impossible than creating a superhero?"

Floyd shrugged. "It's been done," he said. "Superheroes haven't."

"Wait, wait, wait," Kate said quickly. "What do you mean 'it's been done'? Who's done it? When? How?"

Floyd bit his tongue.

"You're one of those space nuts, aren't you," Kate said. "You think there's extraterrestrial life waiting to communicate with us."

Floyd didn't answer.

"And yet," she laughed at him. "And yet you think that creating a superhero is impossible!"

"Well, it is!" he exclaimed.

"And how do you know?" she asked plainly.

Floyd took a deep breath. "Supervillains are created because of a genetic mutation on a very basic level," he explained. "Any time genetics are altered in humans it results in the same genetic mutation. Nobody understands why, but it is the only thing that all super humans have in common. Any superhero you attempt to create will share this basic property, and will therefore also be a supervillain."

"But if we can isolate what it is that makes the villains villainous, and remove it, then we can create a hero," Kate argued.

"It is the mutation that causes the villainy," Floyd said. "Superpowers and villainous intent have the same root cause and cannot be separated."

"But how do you know that?" Kate repeated. "There are plenty of tests that can be performed to determine if the causes cannot be separated. Yours is only one of many untested theories."

"My theory may be untested," Floyd said, "But at least it's safe. My theory won't have laboratory-created villain unleashed in the heart of our scientific communities, where they are more likely to be able to inflict lasting damage."

"Life isn't safe, Floyd," Kate said. "Sometimes you have to take a little risk!"

"You want to play dice with the whole planet?" Floyd accused. "It's your world; go ahead! But don't say I didn't warn you."

The conversation screeched to a halt.

Floyd tried putting his face in his hands and discovered that one was still handcuffed to the table. He tugged at it in frustration.

"I'm sorry," he said distractedly. "I... I was out of line."

Kate rested her chin on one hand. "Does this happen to you often?" she asked.

"Does what happen?" Floyd repeated, puzzled.

"Getting arrested and abandoned in an interrogation room with a curious woman?"

Floyd stared at her in speechless confusion.

"Kate, leave Floyd alone," Joseph said, coming back.

Floyd looked up at him, eager to be rescued.

"Don't worry," Adams said, pulling out the key to the handcuffs. "She does this to everyone. It's not just you."

"You're letting me go?" Floyd asked, rubbing his wrist.

"We sorted things out for you, yes," Adams said. "But you listen to me and listen well."

He grabbed Floyd by the collar and slammed him up against the wall, forcing him to meet his gaze.

"Never pull a stunt like that again," Adams said in a low voice. "Is that absolutely clear?"

Floyd swallowed and nodded.

"Swear it!" Adams shouted. "You stop with the guns, you stay away from the Queen's Guard, and no more terrorist attacks. Understand?"

"I swear," Floyd said desperately. "No terrorist attacks. I'm sorry."

"You keep being sorry and you keep messing up," Adams said, stepping back. "Try harder."

"I'm sorry," Floyd repeated. "What do you want me to do?"

"Come with me," Adams said. "We've got to crack this thing before anyone else dies."

"Were there more murders?" Floyd asked quietly.

"Twelve year old girl named Annie," Adams said. "Killed in broad daylight and no one saw the killer. Come and take a look."

He glanced back at Kate, realising she was still there. "Would you do me a favor and get a wet cloth for his face?" he asked her. "He's still got blood all over it."

"He was cut in the fight," Kate said. "But it's healed up already."

"Yeah, he heals quickly," Adams said unhelpfully. "Come on, Floyd."

"Less worried about him running now?" McCormick asked as they approached.

"I left him locked up with my sister," Adams said. "He's learned his lesson."

"Mind tell me exactly what happened back there?"

Floyd ran his fingers through his hair. "The henchmen are scared," he said. "Terrified, actually. Whoever this guy is, he's made his power clear."

"What power?" McCormick asked. "What kind of—what did you call it? Mastermind?—are we looking for?"

"As scared as the henchmen are?" Floyd said. "He's not paying these guys. He must be controlling them somehow; through telepathy or hypnotism or... something. He's killing for fun. Or, rather, he's watching other people kill. For fun."

"So how do we find this guy and stop him?" McCormick asked.

Floyd sighed. "I'll get you a list of addresses," he said. "I just need a little time."

"No machine guns," Adams said warningly.

"No machine guns," Floyd promised.

"We're running against the clock here," McCormick said. "We know he'll go after another victim in the next 24 hours."

"I know," Floyd said. "Believe me, I know."

Kate came back with a wet cloth and handed it to Floyd, who rubbed it over his face ineffectually. She sighed, reminiscent of a mother of small children, and took it back from him.

"You're missing spots," she said. "Hold still."

They were the same height, and he squirmed under her ministrations, finally resorting to staring at his feet.

"This is my sister Kate," Adams said, introducing her. "Kate, this is Inspector McCormick."

"How do you do?" he said.

"I'm delighted to meet you," Kate said, stepping back to survey her handiwork. She frowned at the blood on the cloth, blood with no injury to have emerged from.

"Give me that," Floyd muttered, snatching it from her.

Kate said nothing else, but her face retained it's thoughtful expression.

"Right then," McCormick said, clapping his hands together. "Everyone to work."

Floyd mumbled an excuse and darted out the front door. McCormick went back to his office. Joseph turned to Kate apologetically.

"I'm sorry," he said. "I'm sure that's not what you had in mind when you wanted to have lunch with me."

"Not at all." She smiled. "I had a most enjoyable time."

She glanced at the door Floyd had just vanished through, and back at her brother. "Who is he?" she asked.

"Floyd?" Joseph feigned surprise. "He's just a reporter."

"That's what he said," she commented. "I don't believe you. Is he... superhuman?"

"Floyd?" Joseph laughed nervously. "No. What gives you that idea? He's just... special," he finished.

"Mmhmm," Kate said. "I want his phone number."

"He's just a reporter," Joseph protested. "He owes me a few favors, that's all."

"He handled himself pretty well today," Kate commented.

"Oh, don't do that," Adams muttered.

"Do what?"

"Admire him," Joseph said. "He thinks highly enough of himself as it is."

"I don't think he's like that," Kate said, frowning.

"You've known him for half a day," her brother replied. "Trust me. You really don't want to get involved with this guy."

"Why?"

"Because he's flighty, and strange, and he's going to get himself killed one of these days."

"Like today?" Kate countered. "He doesn't look dead to me."

"Look, Kate, you have no idea—"

"Then tell me," she interrupted.

"Don't you already have a boyfriend?" Joseph asked, trying to change the subject.

"Bryan?" Kate laughed. "I work with Bryan, and occasionally humour him. It's not like I care."

"And you care about Floyd?" Joseph said dubiously.

Kate shrugged. "He intrigues me," she said. "And he's very brave."

"He's foolhardy," Joseph corrected. "He doesn't take direction or follow orders."

Kate smiled. "Neither do I."

"He's impulsive, and irrational—"

"And everything you can't stand," Kate concluded. "It's like he was designed to irritate you."

She laughed at delight at this realisation, and her brother decided to ignored her.

"I want his number, Joseph," she said firmly.

"He hasn't got one," Joseph retorted.

"What do you mean, he hasn't got one?"

"It's complicated," he stammered. "He calls you, not the other way around."

"That's a strange practice for a writer," Kate observed.

"He works for the London Star," Adams scoffed. "And he barely deserves the title. You should see his stuff. I've seen better written police reports!"

"I'm not interested in him for his writing abilities," Kate pointed out.

"Then why are you interested in him?" Adams demanded.

"If I find out," Kate offered, "I'll let you know."

She snagged a notepad off of the clerk's desk and wrote rapidly on it.

"Give him this," she said.

"Kate," Joseph protested.

"I won't leave you alone unless you promise," she threatened.

"Fine," her brother said. "Just don't say I didn't warn you!"

"Thank you," Kate said with a winning smile. "I'll be in touch, Joseph."

She blew him a kiss and left the station, leaving him staring at the scrap of paper with considerable foreboding.

FRIDAY'S VILLAIN IS LOVING AND GIVING

Floyd showed up bright and early at Scotland Yard, flapping around multiple copies of the same list.

"You look excited," McCormick observed.

"He's got to be one of these guys," Floyd said, passing out copies. "It took all night, but I went through my database and it has to be one of these five."

Adams read the list aloud.

"The Sabre, the Angel of Mercy, Lizard-Man, Unknown, and the Black Shadow. Why these?"

"We know two things about our villain," Floyd explained. "He kills for fun, and he can control other people. So these are people who have aspects of both.

"First we have the Sabre."

Supervillain Name: Sabre
Real Name: Todd something
Superpowers: Speed and accuracy
Appearance: Fierce and Mongolian in style. Black beard and twirly moustache.
Age: 30s
Costume: something reddish that looks highly impractical to fight in.
Currently Located: England
Country of Origin: Unknown
Lair: Unknown
Personality: See below.
Life Story: I really don't feel like asking.
Miscellaneous Details: He likes sharp knives. Very sharp ones. On occasion, he hires other experts to work with him, but these minions seem to come and go. Thrives on violence and blood. Believes in giving everyone an "honourable" death, to the extent of teaching his victims swordplay before killing them. He may or may not actually drink his victim's blood.
Status: At large

"Notice the bit about swords," Floyd said. "He's unlikely to be our killer, but I should check on him anyway. He can manipulate people through fear, and one of these days I should really do something about that..."

He winced at some revived memory, and opened the next profile.

Supervillain Name: Angel of Mercy
Real Name: Dr. Edwin MacDonald
Superpowers: Chemistry manipulation
Appearance: Medium height. Grey hair. Blue-grey eyes.
Age: late fifties
Costume: lab gear
Current Location: Europe
Country of Origin: England
Lair: An abandoned hospital wing.
Personality: Mild-mannered. Gentle. Wants to heal all the hurts of the world.
Life Story: Even as a child, Dr. MacDonald was always deeply affected by the hurts of those around him. He became a doctor to help alleviate those hurts, but as years went by he saw the futility of helping the world to heal. He was involved in a scandal surrounding his involvement in the assisted suicides of several of his patients that led to him having his license to practice medicine revoked. Since the development of his new superpowers he has been working on a supervirus that will wipe out the entire world's population, healing them for once and for all.
Miscellaneous Details: none
Status: At Large

"Last time I checked, this guy was on a mission to end the world through developing the perfect supervirus," Floyd explained. "He wouldn't kill for fun, per se, but there might be a logical reason I'm just not seeing. He has a medical background, and medical backgrounds are wild-cards."

He stared at the next one.

Supervillain Name: Lizard-Man
Real Name: unknown
Superpowers: Giant Lizard
Appearance: Giant Lizard
Age: unknown
Costume: Did you miss the bit about giant lizard?
Geographical Location: Europe
Country of Origin: England
Lair: Sewer system
Personality: reptilian
Life Story: As a kid, he was obsessed with lizards. Then there was an accident of indeterminate type.
Miscellaneous Details: none
Status: At large

"The Lizard-Man..." he hesitated. "Scratch that. He wouldn't do it." He tossed that page aside and went on to the next. "This guy is interesting."

Supervillain Name: Unknown
Real Name: Unknown
Superpowers: Cognitive manipulation
Appearance: Imposing. Probably tall.
Age: unknown
Costume: changes
Geographical Location: Europe
Country of Origin: England
Lair: Unknown
Personality: presumably
manipulative.   Implications   of
aggressiveness.
Life Story: unknown
Miscellaneous Details: none
Status: At large

"That's vague," Adams commented.

"Indeed," Floyd mused. "I don't remember anything about this one. I should try to get more data at any rate."

"How do you collect data on someone who is one long list of unknowns?" McCormick asked.

"You invent a description and start putting the fear of death into henchmen," Floyd said, and read the last profile aloud.

Supervillain Name: The Black Shadow
Real Name: Unknown
Superpowers: Possibly superspeed and heightened senses.
Appearance: Ninja-wannabe
Age: teen
Costume: He dresses in all black, all the time.

Geographical Location: Europe
Country of Origin: England
Lair: Prefers basements of abandoned houses. Reason for this is unknown.
Personality: unknown
Life Story: unknown
Miscellaneous Details: intentionally left blank
Status: At large

"I've been meaning to look up this guy," Floyd said, contemplating the profile. "Something about him doesn't make sense."

"Why is he on your list?" Adams asked.

Floyd shrugged. "I don't know. He just is. Don't question my methods."

"Not questioning," Adams said. "Don't get all defensive."

"So we have a list," McCormick said. "What do we do now?"

"We do nothing," Floyd said. "I go investigate."

"That sounds like an idiotic thing to do," the inspector said.

"I know them," Floyd said. "And they know me. If I catch them at home, with their pants down, so to speak, they'll be too embarrassed to cause trouble."

"And what will you do if you find this villain?" McCormick asked.

"What I did yesterday," Floyd said. "Only without a machine gun."

"Are you sure?" Adams asked. "We're talking about a villain who can manipulate your thoughts. What if he manipulates you, too?"

"You're coming with me," Floyd pointed out. "I'll be fine."

Adams glanced at McCormick for approval.

"As strange as this may sound," the inspector said slowly, "I agree. We have to stop this guy, and this sounds like our best shot. But I don't want anyone else dead. Be careful—both of you."

Floyd laughed, but didn't contradict.

They walked out to the car park together, and as Adams reached into his pocket for his keys, he found the scrap of paper Kate had given him the night before.

"Here," he said, handing it to Floyd.

"What's this?" he asked, frowning.

"Kate's phone number," Adams said. "She wants you to call her."

"Why?"

"It's an expression girls use when they're interested in having a relationship with someone."

Floyd was puzzled. "What kind of relationship?"

"Girlfriend?"

"Oh. I don't have time for a girlfriend."

"You might have to tell her that yourself."

"Why didn't you warn me?" Floyd complained.

"Warn you about what? That I had a sister?"

"That," Floyd said, "and that your sister was... her."

"She's quite a character," Joseph agreed. "If she's bothering you, just tell her to leave you alone."

"I don't—" he broke off. *I don't know what I want*, he had been about to say. But what he wanted was of no consequence. What mattered was problem at hand.

Abruptly, he stuffed the paper in his pocket and put his mind back back where it belonged, on his work.

....

Sabre lived in the lap of luxury, forced out of his patrons at the tip of his very sharp blade. Floyd walked up to his door and knocked without any attempt at subterfuge.

"Aha!" Sabre shouted, recognising him. "I knew you would be back! You shall be punished. At the end of my blade, you shall taste of death!"

As he uttered the last word, blades seemed to shoot out of his fingers, and he was suddenly holding more sharp implements then either Floyd or Adams were comfortable with.

"Put the sharp things down," Floyd said, taking an instinctive step backwards. "I just came to talk."

"What need have we with words? Let our blades do the talking for us! No other information shall I yield to you than the taste of my steel."

"Enough with the references to tasting," Floyd said. "I don't really want to fight with you today; I have better things to do. Just tell me what I want to know and we'll be on our way."

"Under what circumstances shall I lower myself to be your informant?" Sabre demanded. "What cowardly profession would you coerce me to engage in?"

"None! Nothing!" Floyd said in exasperation. "I'm going to kill you sooner or later, so the question is: should it be sooner or later? Because if you're not the villain I'm looking for, then you can live another day or two, but if you won't tell me, then I'm going to kill you for good measure."

He managed to sound confident in his threats, but Adams noticed he didn't take his eyes off one of the longer knives pointed in his direction.

The blades lowered slightly and Sabre squinted, his bushy eyebrows coming even closer together.

"What is it that you desire to know?"

"Where were you between the hours of twelve and six AM Wednesday morning?" Floyd asked.

"Here, practising with my blades. Why?"

"And the morning before?"

"The same."

"And before that?"

"Ah, that morning I was out dancing with a delightful young maiden. She is, alas, deceased. Why do you press me with so many questions?"

"What was her name?"

"Anne Carson. Why?"

"How many minions do you currently employ?"

"Minions?" repeated Sabre in disgust. "You think a master of my calibre would stoop so low as to employ minions?"

"Whatever you call them," Floyd said impatiently.

"I have two novices who study to one day be as great as I am. Why?"

"Where are they?"

"Inside, practising."

"Were they with you here Tuesday and Wednesday morning?"

"Indeed! We have not gone out in several days now."

"In that case," Floyd said, stepping back, "you may continue to practice your art. I will come again."

Sabre grinned, his teeth like little knives jumping out of his mouth. "I look forward to it," he said, and closed the door.

"Couldn't he have been lying?" Adams asked, traipsing after Floyd.

"Could, yes," Floyd said. "But he wasn't."

"How do you know?"

"You get a sense about these things after a while," Floyd explained. "I was pretty sure it wasn't him anyway, but I wanted to check. If he'd turned to serial killings, there would have been some other change about him, something off I would have noticed. There wasn't. It wasn't him."

"We could have at least checked his alibi," Adams protested.

"Waste of time," Floyd said shortly. "And time is short."

....

They stopped next at an old clinic, abandoned who-knew-how-many years ago. The neighbourhood was dead and quiet. The windows were dirty and cracked. The door creaked on rusty hinges when Floyd forced it open.

A breath of freezing cold air hit them as they stepped through the doors. The lights inside were dim. The lobby was empty.

"Creepy," Adams stated.

"Hush," Floyd whispered.

Their shoes clicked on spotless, shining tile floors as they walked towards the back of the building. The soft hum of the air conditioner was the only other sound.

"I'm surprised this place still has electricity," Adams observed.

"Shh," Floyd said sharply.

The doors they passed stood wide open, revealing empty, sterile examination rooms. Everything was dim and looked brand new. Adams started to ask a question and abruptly changed his mind.

The door at the very end of the hall was closed. Floyd rested his hand on it and listened for a moment. He touched the doorknob and decided it was locked. He put a finger on his lips, warning Adams to be silent, and then he kicked the door down.

The noise was startling after the extreme quiet, and Adams half expected to hear alarms and gunfire descend in its wake, but instead there was only the cold clicking of Floyd's footsteps as he stepped over the rubble and into a brightly lit and perfectly white lab room.

Everything was white or silver, from the shoes of the lab assistant to the colour of their instruments. The floor was white tile. The walls and cabinets were all a perfect shade of pure white. Half a dozen men and women in white coats, caps, gloves, and masks looked up in surprise, their hands frozen around their tools in surprise.

"Who is in charge here?" Floyd asked, his voice unnaturally loud.

"I am," one of the men said, stepping forward and taking his mask off. From his crisp white tie to his black, business-like socks he was clearly the superior of the other workers. "Who are you?"

"Jeffry Floyd, special police force," Floyd lied. "State your name and intention."

The doctor squinted down at him. "Who are you?"

"A better question would be, who are you?" Floyd said confidently. "And what are you working on here?"

"Careful, Floyd," Adams said.

"I call myself the Angel of Mercy," the villain said in a quiet voice. "We're working on a very noble cause."

"What's your real name?" Floyd demanded.

"My real name is Dr. Edwin MacDonald. What can I help you with?"

"What are you working on here?"

"I am developing the Ultimate Supervirus," he explained with a smile. "This virus, when it is complete, will be airborne around the world, and eliminate over two thirds of Earth's population."

"I'm sure that will be inconvenient for a lot of people," Floyd observed dryly.

"It will be a glorious day," Dr. MacDonald agreed. "I feel sorry for those who must remain behind."

"Why is that?"

"Life is such a dreary thing, isn't it, Mr. Floyd? It is terrible to be tied here. So many things we cannot do as long as we are confined to these mortal bodies. I will set the human race free, Mr. Floyd. I will let them soar."

"A noble cause indeed," Floyd said sarcastically. "Tell me, have you been doing any work with knives lately?"

"Knives?" said the supervillain, raising his eyebrows. "Such an uncivilised and barbaric method of experimentation, although certain psychological aspects of it does appeal to me. Why do you ask?"

"When was the last time you left this room?"

"Why..." he blinked. "I cannot remember. Perhaps three days. Perhaps more. Is it important?"

"No," Floyd said sharply. "I think we're done here."

"Oh wait," Dr. MacDonald called, as he turned to go. "Floyd..."

Floyd turned back slowly. "What is it?"

"Don't grieve for those you have lost," Dr. MacDonald said with a smile.

"Who are you talking about?"

"The murders. They have gone on to a better place. They have preceded us into a new era where there will be no more dying."

"How do you know about that?" Floyd asked tersely.

"There is no need to grieve," the Angel of Mercy said, still smiling. "You will soon join them when my work is complete."

"Is that a fact?" Floyd snapped, taking a step forward. "How do you know about the murders?"

Dr. MacDonald smiled enigmatically and didn't answer the question.

"I'll kill you," Floyd hissed. "I will—"

"Enough, Floyd," Adams interrupted. "We have important things to do."

"Enjoy your time on Earth," the Angel of Mercy whispered. "I'll see you on the other side."

As they left the room, Floyd felt the words echo in the back of his mind and, without understanding why, he was afraid.

....

They spent the rest of the afternoon kicking in the doors on empty houses, only to find the basements even more empty. Floyd got more grumpy and less certain with every building they inspected, keeping up a running stream of excuses why his first guess had been wrong, and his second, and his third, and his—

"No one's making any accusations," Adams interrupted. "You haven't done anything wrong."

Floyd stopped mid-sentence. "You don't think I'm being incompetent or losing my touch?" he said.

"No," Adams said. "Why would I think that?"

"I don't know," Floyd mumbled. "I'm used to working alone, that's all."

He kicked in the door to the basement stairs with unnecessary glee.

"It was probably unlocked," Adams observed. Floyd ignored him.

From the bottom of the stairs came a cry of protest.

Floyd ran down the stairs, Adams close behind, and stared in amazement at the scene that confronted him.

In the middle of the room, surrounded by computer equipment, sat an extremely nerdy teenager, all in black, complete with wide-rimmed glasses. A black sofa was along one wall, and geeky posters were taped at odd angles above it. The floor was covered with cables of all sorts twisting like snakes around the feet of the invaders.

"Who are you?" Floyd demanded.

"I am The Black Hacker," the teenager said in a sinister voice.

Floyd stared. "The what?"

"The Black Hacker," he cackled, and spread out his fingers in a menacing manner over the keyboard. "I am developing the Ultimate Supervirus," he said triumphantly.

"Oh, that," Floyd said dismissively.

"What do you know about it?" the nerd said indignantly. "Who are you people anyway?"

"I know about it," Floyd said, "because you're not the first person to try to do it. And it's completely impossible."

"I will succeed!" the kid yelped, "if you don't destroy everything in here first. Move your feet, mister!" he finished, addressing Adams. The policeman took an instant step backwards.

"What's your name?" Floyd asked.

"I told you. I am the Black—"

"I got that part," Floyd interrupted. "Suppose you tell me your real name."

A sly look came over the nerd's face. "Tell me yours first."

Floyd frowned. "That's irrelevant."

"You're the one trespassing in my space," the Black Hacker accused.

Floyd glanced down at the paper in his hand. "Wait, wait, wait," he said. "You're the Black Hacker?"

"That's what I said," the kid sighed. "Are you deaf?"

"Is your name Steve Kelly?"

"Yes! Wait—how do you know that?"

"You're not the Black Shadow?"

"The what? I've never heard of that."

Floyd crumpled up the page and threw it on the floor. "So much for my database," he muttered. "Let's go."

"I'm confused," Adams said.

"Wait," Kelly said, jumping to his feet. "You're the dude with the database! I do know you. You're the one looking for the Manipulator, right?"

Floyd stopped. "The who?"

"The Manipulator," Kelly said. "You think he's behind those murders."

He picked up one of the papers Floyd had discarded and handed it to him. "This guy," he said.

Floyd stared at the page marked "Unknown."

"How do you know I'm looking for him?" he asked uneasily.

"Oh, everyone knows it," Kelly said. "The Manipulator thinks you're too much trouble. You're standing in the way of his progress, and he wants you removed."

"Like that's anything new," Floyd muttered. "Tell me about the Manipulator. Why is he called that? How is he committing the murders?"

"Sorry," Kelly said. "I don't know, and even if I did, I wouldn't tell you. He'd find out and tch. My life would be over."

"I could do terrible things to you," Floyd threatened.

"Yeah," Kelly said defiantly. "But he could do worse. After all, you're human. You have some moral compunctions against attacking an unarmed and defenceless person. But he..." he broke off with a shudder.

"Let's get out of here," Floyd said shortly, and left the basement.

....

"He knew too much about you," Adams observed.

"He knew too much period," Floyd said irritably.

"Well, where are you going next?"

"I don't know," Floyd sighed. "I don't know how to find this Manipulator fellow, or how to fight him even if I do..."

"You should have tried harder to get that Kelly fellow to talk."

"No, I couldn't," Floyd said. "He's right, I wouldn't torture him, and he'd never talk willingly. None of them will. This villain has a pretty strong control on them."

"I still think that Sabre isn't in the clear," Adams said. "His story seemed fishy at best."

"I said that if he were responsible there would be signs," Floyd said irritably. "And anyway, that Kelly fellow cleared up our mysterious' villain's identity for us. He would never have been so afraid of a sword-wielding bully."

"If you say so," Adams said, still not convinced.

"I do," Floyd said shortly. "But I still don't understand. Where is he?"

"Huh?"

"Haven't you noticed? No one else is dead."

"I have noticed that," Adams said. "It makes a nice change."

"No, it doesn't," Floyd said grimly. "I want to know why. I don't like the options."

"Go home and get some rest," Adams told him. "That's what I'm going to do."

Floyd sighed. "It's like everyone knows something I don't," he complained. "And while I'm stumbling around trying to figure out the basic premise of the game, people are dying."

"No one has died all day," Adams said consolingly. "Let's just give it a night and see what we're up against tomorrow, all right?"

Floyd sighed again. "All right," he said finally. "All right. I'll call you in the morning."

"You do that," Adams said, and they went their separate ways.

....

Floyd went home, and read through his database again, picking through entries with inhuman thoroughness. He sorted through the mountains of unfiled notes on supervillains, hints dropped by henchmen, and incomplete database entries. After hours of futile searching, he wrote down everything he knew about the case so far, hoping to see some connection he already knew didn't exist.

Sometime around midnight, he sat down in the middle of the wreck he'd made of his apartment and stared at a scrap of paper with nothing but a string of numbers and the words 'call me' scrawled across it.

"I don't have time for a girlfriend," he muttered, but a voice in his head was laughing at him, stirring up things he hadn't felt for years. And finally he picked up the phone and dialled.

"Ah, Mr. Floyd," said a silky smooth voice on the other end of the line. "I was told you might call."

Floyd frowned. He'd heard that voice somewhere. "Who told you that?" he demanded. "Who is this?"

"I hear you're looking for me," said the man on the other end of the line. "Well, now you can come find me, or Kate Adams will die."

Phone and paper fell to the floor, and the villain on the other end was satisfied to hear the slam of a door before the line went dead.

Inspector Floyd

SATURDAY'S HEROES
WORK HARD
FOR A LIVING

Floyd went out into the dark with no idea of where he was going. He ran, and he walked, and he sat alone on rooftops, staring at the city below, and he came no closer to answering the riddle. He tried to approach the question rationally, and not think about Kate's green eyes—eyes so much like her brother's and yet so different. He tried to clear his head and logically deduce why the Manipulator would have kidnapped her. He tried to think of who he might get information from on where she was being held.

He tried to separate fact from fancy and truth from fiction, and the only place it got him was the most popular haunt of evil henchmen.

They fell silent when he walked through the door, but his only comment was to the barkeeper, and they all relaxed. One henchman, called Snakey, with skin covered with hideous black and orange tattoos, decided that Floyd was distracted enough to be a target.

"What are you brooding about?" he leered.

Floyd glared and didn't answer.

"Did you lose a battle? Or, I know..." he grinned around the room. "It's a woman, right? That's the sort of brooding look that goes along with rejection."

To Snakey's disappointment, Floyd didn't rise to the bait.

"You know what you should do?" the henchman asked, slinking closer. "You should go back to her and put her in her place, you know? Stand up to her, and show her that she can't toss you out. Show her what a man you are."

The henchmen tittered because they all knew that Floyd was no more human than they were.

Floyd met his antagonist's eyes briefly, but his thoughts were far away and he didn't respond.

Another henchman slunk over, eager to join the fun. He was small and black, with tiny white eyes that peered out of his indistinguishable face.

"Ooooh, does the unconquerable Floyd have relationship problems?" Blacky cackled with laughter. "You could bring her down here, 'rescue her' a few times, and see if she can turn you down then."

Floyd glanced at him briefly, eyes narrowed in irritation.

"And if she does," Blacky added, laughing gleefully, "You can just leave her here and let us handle her for you!"

"The Manipulator," Floyd said abruptly. Silence fell over the group.

"You want to talk?" he said threateningly. "Start talking about him."

The henchmen began to shift away from him uneasily. Floyd reached out, quick as a flash, and caught Blacky by the throat.

"Start talking," he hissed.

"I don't know nothing," he croaked. "I swear I don't."

"You're sure ignorant all of a sudden," Floyd said derisively. "A moment ago you were just full of information and advice."

"Listen," Snakey said, inching closer. "You gotta understand. None of us know anything about the Manipulator. That's the best information we can give you."

"You know that you don't know anything?" Floyd repeated. "That's supposed to be helpful, how?"

"Think about it," Snakey said, patting him on the shoulder. "It will come to you."

"Wait a minute," Floyd said, releasing Blacky and catching Snakey's arm as he tried to walk away. "Wait a minute..."

Pieces settled and fell into place.

"Camoflaughe," Floyd said. "You don't know anything about him because he never shows his true self! You mislead me. You shouldn't call him the Manipulator, he should be the Chameleon!"

"Something like that," Snakey said, extricating himself.

"He uses human subjects to commit his crimes," Floyd continued, not noticing. "He manipulates those around him into believing what he wants them to believe. He finds somewhere to blend in, somewhere inconspicuous..."

"Now you're catching on," Snakey said appreciatively.

"He's hiding in plain sight," Floyd said, and all the pieces fell into place.

....

The clinic was every bit as cold as Floyd remembered it, but now it was even darker. The building was silent, and empty. Only the hum of the air conditioner kept a monotonous tone going in the background. Floyd stepped cautiously into the hall, scarcely breathing. The doors were still open, silent, and empty. The door to the lab at the end of the hall was closed. Everything was exactly the same as it was the first time Floyd saw it, only so much different.

The door swung open without a squeak. A clock on the wall declared the time to be after midnight. The lab wasn't empty, but it was still. The lab assistants lay on the floor, unmoving. Their equipment lay shattered around them. No one was left alive.

Floyd moved among them quickly and efficiently verifying that they were all dead, and had been so for hours. They must have been killed shortly after he'd left the building earlier that day.

"So we meet," a voice said, shattering the silence. Floyd whirled around to face the speaker behind him. A tall, dark haired man seemed to fill the open doorway, and the smirk on his face was more foreboding than many a villain's sneer. "Tell me, Floyd. How did you find me?"

"You made a mistake," Floyd said. "When I was here yesterday."

"And what would that be?"

"Your socks," Floyd said, pointing. "Your socks were black, not white. You hadn't had time to change them."

"That was enough?" the villain said dubiously.

"The real Angel of Mercy would have never made that kind of mistake," Floyd said. "I doubt he even owned black socks."

"And yet his identity managed to shield me for quite some time," the villain said. "Very good work, Mr. Floyd. Any other observations?"

"Oh, I have it all figured out," Floyd said confidently. "You killed supervillains, and then stole their identity. You had the henchmen so confused they didn't know what they were dealing with. They didn't discover the bodies until days after the murder occurred. You were a ghost, a shadow, and a nameless dread. You kidnapped humans off the street and manipulated them to do your bidding; hence your moniker. You could use a different killer for every murder, making your actions untraceable. Right so far?"

"Impressive," the Manipulator said mildly.

"It's a very neat setup," Floyd said. "I just have one question: why? What's the point?"

"I'm a supervillain," said the Manipulator. "Do I need a reason?"

"It's rather elaborate to not have a specific point," Floyd said.

"What can I say?" the villain said, spreading his hands. "I like watching humans die."

Floyd's eyes hardened. "What's your name?" he demanded. "Your real name."

The supervillain laughed then, and his laugh was as cold as the icy air washing through the vents in the lab.

"I think I'll ask the questions," he said, finally recovering himself.

"No," Floyd said instantly. "I ask the questions. What do you call yourself?"

"I've never needed a name," the villain said. "My servants call me Master, and that is sufficient."

"I'm not your servant," Floyd said hotly.

"You will be."

"I don't think so."

The villain held up a warning finger. "Look at me," he said, his voice silky and venomous at the same time.

"I am looking at you," Floyd snapped. "And I see a murderer. You're going to die today, villain."

"I didn't kill those people," the villain said, still keeping his voice smooth. "I can prove I was nowhere near them when they died."

"You're not going to prove anything," Floyd said. "You're guilty. I've decreed it."

"Who makes you my judge?" the villain asked.

"I do," Floyd said swiftly. "Judge, jury, and executioner."

"Aren't there laws against such things?"

"Not for supervillains," Floyd said with finality.

"Wait," the villain said, dropping his attempt to manipulate Floyd.

"This conversation is over," Floyd said firmly.

"Hear me out," the villain protested.

"You have nothing to say that could possibly interest me."

"Oh, I think I do," the villain said, with a smooth smile. "Have you forgotten about Kate?"

He had forgotten about Kate.

"Kill me," the villain continued, "and she dies."

It took Floyd ten seconds to make a decision. "Even if that were true," he sneered, "and it's not, it doesn't matter. Killing you is my first priority."

Joseph would never speak to him again if he knew.

The villain looked surprised. "I thought surely you cared about saving her life?" he said.

"Who's going to care about carrying out your orders once you're dead?" Floyd asked. "I care about doing my job. Now are we going to stand around chattering all night or do you have some death trap you're going to spring?"

"Oh, I have a better idea," said the Manipulator. "I want you to come work for me."

Floyd laughed. "That's never going to happen," he sneered.

"Why not?" asked the villain. "You want to kill supervillains don't you?"

"I don't want to," Floyd retorted. "I do."

"I do as well," said the Manipulator. "You've seen what I'm capable of. You know that I'm eliminating competition. You know that we're really working towards the same goal."

"No, we're not," Floyd snapped. "You kill people! And-and Stabby! What's the deal with that, huh? I liked that kid!"

"You liked a henchmen?" laughed the villain.

"He was a sweet kid!" Floyd protested. "Sure, he had an evil streak but... he was useful."

"You would have had to kill him eventually," the Manipulator said. "When he grew up, he would have been a powerful enemy. I saved you the trouble."

"I don't need anyone to save me trouble!" Floyd shouted. "It was my right to kill him, no one else's. And you're still a murderer."

"You can't prove it."

"This isn't a courtroom. I don't need to prove it. I know."

"We could work out a deal," the villain offered. "The killings could stop."

"And I'd still kill you," Floyd said swiftly.

"Ah, but then who would take out the supervillains?" he asked, his voice regaining it's silky overtones. "Aren't you tired of doing it all yourself? Wouldn't you like an ally?"

Floyd glanced around the dark lab nervously. There were no other villains in sight. He could take out the Manipulator with hardly any effort, but he didn't make a move.

"I don't make deals with villains," he said, but his voice lacked conviction.

"You don't have to make a deal. Just look the other way."

"No."

"Listen to reason, Floyd. Yes, I killed some. But were there really any more deaths then the villains I removed would have caused? The less villains there are the less people will get hurt. Eventually there won't be anyone at all except for you and me, and the streets of London will be peaceful and safe again."

Floyd laughed hollowly. "Safe from everyone but you," he said. "And what will you do? Force them to fight in gladiatorial games? Paint the entire city a different shade of red each morning?"

"My motives are purely peaceful, I assure you."

"You're a villain. Your motives are pure evil."

"You can't prove that."

"People are dead."

"More than that are alive because of me."

"You're trying to mess with my head," Floyd said with defiance he didn't feel. "It won't work."

"It's working already. Look at me, Floyd."

"No," Floyd said, shaking his head, and staring determinedly at the floor. "No. You're going to die. This is going to end here and now."

"I could save you so much trouble."

"No."

"Yes," the villain whispered, coming closer. "Yes."

"No," Floyd said, his words beginning to slur together. "No. You... you're a villain."

"So are you, Floyd."

"No," he repeated. "I'm a... I..."

"You kill, too."

"Not innocent people."

"If you had to, you would."

"No," he protested feebly. "Just... just the villains. The supervillains," he added for clarification, looking up suddenly.

He clung to the door frame feeling confused and disoriented. The villain smiled kindly at him, and he felt himself suddenly desperate to please this impressive, towering figure before him. What had he said he was called...

"Master," he whispered.

"That's it," the villain said, smiling with pleasure. "We'll work together, won't we, Floyd?"

"I'd like that," he stammered hoarsely.

"We'll rule the world?"

"No," Floyd said. "The galaxy."

The villain laughed. "Yes," he said. "The galaxy. And you'll help me."

"I would... be honored."

"You're a good boy, Floyd."

"Thank you... Master."

"You look tired, Floyd."

"I am. It's been... a long day."

"Sleep now," the villain instructed. "Go to sleep and rest, and when you wake up we'll talk again."

Floyd nodded, suddenly unable to keep his eyes open.

"Sleep," the villain whispered. "Everything is going to be fine."

....

The phone call came at four in the morning.

"You have a lot to lose," a sinister voice hissed in Adams' ear. "Your sister... your friend..."

"Who is this?" Adams asked, irritated and sleepy.

"Your friend called me the Manipulator," the voice said, enunciating carefully. "Now he calls me Master."

"Master?" Adams said, confused. "What are you talking about?"

"Floyd is in my service now," the Manipulator explained.

"I still don't understand."

"If you want to see your sister alive again I suggest you return to the clinic as soon as possible."

"What clinic?"

"The one you searched yesterday afternoon. Where the Angel of Mercy had his headquarters."

"And you have my sister there?"

"And your friend."

"You mean Floyd?"

"Yes. He's here, too."

"Let me get this straight," Adams said, scratching his head. "You're inviting me to come rescue them? I haven't read Floyd's list of Stupid Things Supervillains do, but I'm pretty sure that's near the top."

The evil voice chuckled in amusement. "Oh no, I'm not proposing you should attempt to rescue them. That would be foolish indeed. I'm inviting you to come and watch them die."

"Oh."

"I want to see the look on your face when you lose those most dear to you."

"I'll be down in ten minutes."

"Sergeant Adams," the voice said warningly, "I suggest you come alone."

Adams hung up.

....

When Adams got to the clinic, it was empty. He hurried through the silent corridor and flung open the door to the lab in the back, but no one jumped out to greet him.

The lab was dark and the light switch didn't work. He pulled out his flashlight and shone it around, revealing the bodies of the lab assistants. One of them made a muffled moaning sound and he shone the light to reveal Kate, bound and gagged on the floor. Hastily, he untied her.

"Where's the villain?" he asked. "Where's Floyd?"

"It's a trap," Kate said. "Floyd is over there."

Adams was next to him in a flash.

"Floyd," he whispered. "Come on, Floyd. We've got to get out of here."

Floyd moaned incoherently and shielded his eyes from the light.

"Come on," Adams repeated urgently. "We have to go."

"It's a trap," Kate repeated, joining them. "If we try to leave, we'll be killed."

"Come on, Floyd," Adams said, slapping him. "Wake up. We need you."

"Where am I?" Floyd mumbled. "What happened?"

"You're in the clinic," Adams said. "Where the Angel of Mercy was holed up? Kate was kidnapped, you came to rescue her. Do you know what happened after that?"

Floyd frowned. "There was a villain," he said. "I don't... I don't remember."

"They must have him drugged or something," Joseph said. "Let's get him outside."

Kate looked worried, but she helped her brother haul Floyd to his feet and carry him back down the hallway to the exit. They stepped out onto the concrete front steps and were immediately blinded by multiple pairs of headlights.

"You were faster than expected!" a voice Adams recognized from the telephone spoke from somewhere beyond the glare.

"What do you want?" Adams demanded.

"I told you," the villain said. "I want to watch you all die. Floyd," he called. "Wake up. I need your help."

"You leave him alone," Kate snapped in a no-nonsense voice.

"You think you have more control over him than me?" the villain asked. "By all means. Be my guest. See if you can convince him not to kill you both."

"Put him down," Kate ordered, and they lowered Floyd onto the steps.

"Listen to me, Floyd," Kate said, looking into his eyes. "This man is controlling you. You can't let him. You have to help us, understand?"

"Listen to the lady," the Manipulator taunted. "Wake up and help me."

"Listen to me," Kate pleaded. "Floyd, listen to me. Please."

He stared at her through dark, uncomprehending eyes. "I don't... I don't know you," he said finally, the words slurring together.

"Yes, you do," Kate said insistently. "We met the day before yesterday. I'm Kate Adams, Joseph's sister. You know Joseph. You've known him for years."

"No," he shook his head. "I don't... remember."

"Floyd?" the villain said, his voice ingratiating.

"You shut up," Adams said harshly.

"Let me..." Floyd said, trying to stand.

"Wake up, Floyd," the villain said. "I need your help."

"He's manipulating him," Kate protested. "Joseph, you've got to do something!"

"I don't know what I'm supposed to do," Adams protested. "He's the supervillain expert."

"What his first name?" Kate asked desperately.

"Uh, it's Jeffry," her brother said uncertainly.

"Jeffry," Kate said, shaking him. "Listen to me, Jeffry. You've got to get control of yourself, understand?"

"Floyd," the villain said. "Catch."

Something sharp and silver flashed in the light as it hurtled towards the trio clustered on the steps. Kate stumbled back just in time, and Floyd reached out and caught the knife.

"Floyd," Adams said without conviction. "Give me that."

He stepped forward and put his hand firmly on Floyd's shoulder. "You don't want to do this," he said calmly.

Without warning, Floyd's left hand came out of nowhere and socked him in the jaw. Before he could recover, Floyd hit him again and then kicked him in the stomach, sending him tumbling down the stairs. Kate darted forward to kneel beside her brother, glancing up in alarm at Floyd.

He stood motionless with the knife in his hand, his eyes blank and his face expressionless— a robot awaiting orders.

"That's good," the villain said. "That's very good. Now I have a little job for you, Floyd. Are you ready?"

"Yes, Master," he said.

"Oh, for crying out loud!" Kate exclaimed. "Master? How did you fall for that, Floyd?"

"Very good, Floyd," the villain said companionably. "Now I want you to kill Kate Adams. Slowly. Is that clear?"

....

Floyd stood frozen, conscious only of the fact that there was a knife in his hands. A voice was giving him a command, a familiar voice, one that demanded obedience. It was similar and yet not the same as a voice he remembered in training, and he knew that to disobey would only cause him grief in the long run.

But there was a second voice, arguing with the first voice, and it was like nothing he could remember hearing before, but still familiar.

"Listen to me, Floyd. Try to remember. You're under his control."

"Kill Kate Adams, Floyd. Do you understand?"

"We met on Thursday. You defeated a glassman, and Joseph arrested you. Remember Joseph?"

"Kill Kate Adams, Floyd. Do you understand?"

Other voices started to chime in with their opinions. Some of them weren't there at all. They were voices from the past and they got all mixed in with the voices of the present.

"Does this happen to you often?"

"Does what happen?"

Kill Kate...

"You kill, too."

"Listen to me, Floyd! Floyd!"

There were too many voices giving conflicting orders. Floyd made up his mind and his grip tightened on the scalpel.

....

"What is he doing?" Kate hissed.

"I don't know," Adams said. "I really don't."

"He's cutting himself," Kate said, gripping her brother's arm. "Why is he doing that?"

Adams looked. Floyd closed his hand over the blade and twisted it, and they could see the trickle of blood between his fingers.

"He's activating the nanobots," Adams explained.

"What does that mean?" Kate asked.

"He knows he's not in control," Adams said.

The villain realised it too, and his voice took on a nervous tone.

"Floyd," he said nervously. "Listen to me, Floyd."

Floyd stared at the blood on his fingers, listening to no one.

"You won't kill me," the villain repeated. "You wouldn't just kill me in cold blood. It's not in your nature. You can't destroy an unarmed man."

Floyd glanced up sharply, and his eyes glinted with hatred.

"I wouldn't be so sure," he snapped.

"Floyd," the villain said, panicking. "Listen to—"

He broke off mid sentence, because the knife in his throat made it hard to talk.

Floyd looked down at the blood on his fingers, and then he looked up at Kate and Joseph who stood arm in arm, staring at him. And then he fainted.

BUT THE WOMAN YOU MEET ON THE SABBATH DAY...

The sun was just rising and already it had been the weirdest day in Kate Adams' life. Everything she knew, or thought she knew, about herself, about life, and about the universe in general had been completely upset, turned over, reverted, turned inside out, upside down, and backwards. She had helped her brother capture a serial killer, who turned out to be a supervillain, who could control the thoughts and actions of free-willed people, who had then captured her to lure her brother and his strange friend into his trap, and had then been rescued by said friend who turned out to be...

"An alien?" Kate repeated in astonishment. "From another planet?"

"That's what he says," Adams said, focusing on driving. "And I haven't seen any reason to not believe him."

"You've seen evidence that he's not a nutcase?" Kate demanded.

"Sure," her brother argued. "Did you see what he did back there?"

"I'm really not sure what he did back there," Kate admitted.

"He's been trained to fight supervillains," Adams said. "He threw a knife into that villain's throat because that's what he's been trained to do."

"But he was under the Manipulator's control," Kate said uncertainly.

"Yeah, but he broke out of it somehow. You'd have to ask him how he did it."

"And he's going to be okay? He's not still being... manipulated?"

"The death of the villain should have broken his control," Adams explained. "In fact, the shock of it is probably part of what knocked him out."

"And you're sure we shouldn't take him to a hospital?"

"Kate, what do you think they'd do to an alien at a hospital?" Adams asked patiently.

Kate sighed and turned around to watch the road. "I guess you're right," she said. "It's just... it's all so unusual."

"Floyd has that effect on people."

"Is that even his real name? Floyd?"

Adams shrugged. "It's the only name he's ever given me."

Kate glanced back at the alien in the back seat. Sleeping, he looked as helpless as a child. Whatever his subconscious thoughts were, they were not peaceful ones.

"Do you trust him?" Kate asked, suddenly turning her scrutiny on her brother.

"Oh, don't do that," Adams said, rolling his eyes.

"Do what?"

"That's the question you always ask when you introduce me to a new boyfriend," her brother said, smacking the steering wheel deliberately. "Kate—he's not even human!"

"He is cute," Kate smirked. "But seriously. I've seen what he asks you to do, and I don't want you to get killed. Do you trust him?"

Adams sighed. "I know I shouldn't," he said. "He's dangerous, he's emotionally unstable, and he's more than a little crazy. But yes, I do trust him."

"How much do you trust him?" Kate pressed.

"With my life. And with the safety of Earth."

"And that's why he's here? To defend Earth?"

"That's what he says."

"That's a big job for one person," Kate said softly.

"A very big job," Adams agreed. "But he's our only hope."

"It's that bad?"

Her brother nodded, and the gesture spoke more than words.

"He's that good?"

"He's incredibly good."

"Where are you going?" Kate asked, squinting at the road.

"I'm taking him home," Adams said. "Then I'm taking you to wherever you belong. And then I have to go down to the station and fill out a report. It's going to be a long day."

He yawned.

Kate rubbed his shoulder sympathetically.

"When are you going back to Wales?" Joseph asked.

"I'll go tomorrow," Kate said. "They won't miss me one more day, and I want to see this out to the end."

"I hope we didn't ruin your trip. I'm sure being kidnapped was not part of the itinerary."

She smiled gently. "It's been marvelous," she assured him. "Thank you."

"If you think getting kidnapped by a supervillain is marvelous," Joseph mumbled.

"It is," she said, grinning. "As long as there are heroes like you to come rescue me."

....

Inspector McCormick was not used to having his cases solved for him in the middle of the night, by strange consultants and the sister of one of his Sergeants.

"So you found the killer..." he said slowly.

"Yes sir."

"And he's dead?"

"Yes sir."

"And Floyd killed him?"

"With a knife through the throat, sir."

"He must be very good with a knife," McCormick observed dryly.

"He's very good with just about anything," Adams confirmed.

"So it would seem," McCormick agreed. "So it would seem. We might have to bring him in on some of our other cases sometime."

"I think we could talk him into it," Adams said.

"Thank him officially from the department, would you?" McCormick said, passing a check across the desk. "He did good work last night. And I hope he recovers well."

"He'll appreciate it," Adams said. "I'll make sure I pass the message along."

"What does he do?" McCormick asked. "For a living, usually?"

"He works as a journalist," Adams said, "and he hates it."

McCormick chuckled. "We can change that," he said. "I think we can definitely change that."

....

The supervillain problem had been a super problem for everyone all over the world ever since it began. At first people denied it was happening. Then they panicked about what was happening. Finally, they resorted to pretending that what was happening wasn't happening and went on with their daily lives. They settled down to live their lives normally, made minor adjustments to accommodate their superhuman neighbors, and generally hoped the phenomena would die out eventually, and the world would go back to normal.

It didn't, of course.

It's amazing how well people can immerse themselves in this sort of make-believe. The entire front wall of your house was smashed by two supervillains fighting it out? Oh well, it must have been some thugs with baseball bats. Something should really be done about the youth today. You were kidnapped and held in a dank, wet dungeon for weeks? Your captors confused you with someone else. Oh, and that bank that got robbed last week? Something really must be done about the gang activity. What? They only took one safety deposit box? Well, that's very odd indeed. There must have been some kind of terrible mix-up. It's going to be a nice day, don't you think?

And because of this general denial of the problem, most people made no changes to their daily procedures to accommodate them. This made any kind of reporting system incredibly complicated. 'Supervillains' wasn't an option on the drop down menu.

This applied especially to police work, and Adams spent the remainder of his Saturday arguing with computer programs that didn't like "The Manipulator" as the name of the criminal deemed responsible for the deaths of eight people.

It was almost six o'clock when he wrapped things up and went home, detouring to drop by Floyd's flat.

The alien was up and sitting miserably in front of his computer, cradling a cup of tea that had gone cold long ago.

"How are you doing?" Adams asked, clearing off a part of the sagging sofa.

Floyd shrugged, no longer surprised at the sergeant appearing in his home unannounced.

Adams made himself comfortable and waited.

"I almost did it," Floyd said finally, his voice barely audible. "I almost killed her."

"But you didn't," Adams said. "That's the important part."

"He controls people through his voice," Floyd kept explaining, oblivious to any comments, finally finding relief in talking. "That's how it works. He's not telepathic, and each victim takes special attention; he can't control more than one at a time. If I hadn't gone in there alone, it wouldn't have happened."

His hands trembled and he tightened his grip around the cracked mug he was holding.

"It was stupid," he said vehemently. "It was stupid and impulsive and it almost cost a life."

"You take risks all the time," Adams pointed out. "Why are you so upset over this one?"

"He was controlling me!" Floyd exclaimed. "I called him..." he trailed off, unable to bring himself to utter the word. "He made me do things I would never have done."

"No, he didn't," Adams said. "You won. Remember that."

"I didn't even know if it would work."

"You never know if anything will work."

"Why are you so determined to exonerate me?" Floyd exploded. "Usually you're doing the scolding!"

"Usually you're cocky and unrepentant," Adams countered. "And... you did a good job, Floyd. You stopped a serial killer, you defeated a villain under difficult circumstances, and you saved my sister's life."

"I saved her from myself," Floyd snapped.

"No," Adams shook his head. "She would have died if you hadn't been there, Floyd. The villain could have manipulated me to do it and I wouldn't have been able to resist. So stop blaming yourself."

"He wanted to scare me," Floyd whispered. "He was taunting me the whole time."

"They're starting to figure out that you're a threat," Adams agreed. "Be careful."

Floyd sighed and finally drank his tea, only to make a face when he realised it was cold.

"Give me that," Adams said, taking it away from him. "This should cheer you up instead."

He handed him the check from Inspector McCormick and Floyd stared at it, uncomprehending.

"What is this for?" he asked.

"Consulting fee," Adams explained. "I told you. You did good work today."

Floyd stared in disbelief.

"McCormick was very impressed," Adams added, "which isn't easily done. This might be an alternative to working at the London Star, you know."

Floyd put his face in his hands.

"Take care of yourself," Adams said, putting a hand on his shoulder. "And thank you."

....

When you're accustomed to seeing someone at a specific time in a specific place regularly, it's a bit strange to run into them somewhere else. It's almost like they're a different person. Meeting Adams for lunch on a Sunday at the train station made Floyd feel a little uneasy, like the world was at risk of imploding. But then Kate caught his eye and smiled, and he thought maybe that wouldn't be such a bad way for the world to end, when it came down to it.

"Hi, Floyd," she said brightly. "I'm glad you made it."

"Sorry I'm late," Floyd mumbled.

"Sit," Kate ordered. "Are you feeling all right?"

"I'm fine," Floyd said dismissively.

Kate put her chin in the palm of one hand and regarded him thoughtfully.

"My brother says you're an alien," she said.

"Can't trust you with anything," Floyd said, glaring at Adams.

"He said if I wanted the details I'd have to ask you," Kate offered.

Floyd sighed. "What do you want to know?" he asked softly.

Kate seized her opportunity without regret. "How do you heal so quickly?" she asked.

"I have nanobots in my blood stream designed to repair any damage I might suffer," he said. "Minor injuries heal without a trace."

"Fascinating," Kate said breathlessly.

"I suppose so," Floyd said. "You're the only person who knows besides Joseph, and I'd rather it stay that way."

"I'm sorry," Kate laughed. "I didn't mean to treat you like a specimen. There's a lot more to fascinate me then just the fact that you're apparently immune to injury."

Floyd didn't answer, caught off guard.

"So, yesterday..." Kate said cautiously. "With the Manipulator..."

Caught in a sense of responsibility, Floyd felt obliged to answer.

"Activating the bots in my system also brought their attention to my... altered mental state," he stammered. "They... intervened."

"Clever bots," Kate smiled.

"I suppose so."

"You were very brave," Kate said softly, putting her hand over his. "Thank you."

"I couldn't very well do otherwise," Floyd said, "if I ever hoped to look your brother in the eye again."

"Yes," she laughed and leaned back. "You two are quite a pair."

"What do you do exactly?" Floyd asked curiously, trying to make conversation.

Kate laughed. "That," she said, "is none of your business, Jeffry Floyd."

"How do you know my first name?" he demanded.

Kate shrugged. "Joey told me."

"Of course he did." Floyd glared at him.

"Hey, everyone has to have a nickname," Kate teased.

"It's not a nickname," Floyd argued. "It's my full name."

"No, your full name is Jeffry Lewis Floyd."

"You know that, too."

"Of course I do," she smiled mysteriously. "I even know that you've been offered a chance to be a real police consultant."

"Me?" Floyd grinned and shook his head. "I'd make a terrible cop."

Adams shrugged. "You could change."

"I've been changed enough for one life time, thank you very much," Floyd said grimly.

"Speaking of change," Kate said, gracefully changing the subject. "I checked your website, and I noticed that the Manipulator has his own entry now. Decided to stick with the name?"

"It's all I've got," Floyd said. "He didn't talk."

"Is that unusual?"

"Usually you can't get them to shut up."

Kate laughed. "Talkativeness is a side effect of being a supervillain?" she inquired.

"No," Floyd corrected. "Talkativeness is a sign of insanity. Insanity is a side effect of being a supervillain."

"So when I can't get you to shut up..." Adams suggested.

"Shut up," Floyd growled.

"It's been quite a weekend," Kate observed, checking her watch. "Does this happen to you often?"

The reprise of their earlier conversation caught Floyd off guard, and he didn't answer.

"I'd like to see you again sometime," Kate said. "I know Cardiff is a long way away..."

"I don't have time for a girlfriend," Floyd blurted out.

"I didn't say..." Kate said with an awkward smile.

"Listen to me," Floyd said bluntly. "You know who I am. You know what I do. People who are around me get hurt. You were kidnapped because of me. You almost died because of me. And if I have any respect for you at all, I can only say one thing: stay away from me. I am not a human being, and I am not a being worth knowing."

Kate stared. Her brother's face had "I told you so" written all over it.

"I live in Wales," she said finally. "We don't have much of a supervillain problem there. Experts think it has something to do with the weather. If you ever want a vacation or need someone to talk to, please, give me a call."

She set her card on the table and stood, closing her purse smartly.

"It was so nice to see you again, Joseph."

And with that she was well and truly gone.

Floyd stared, unable to comprehend.

"She didn't listen to me," he said finally. "Does she not believe me?"

"That's Kate for you," Adams said. "Do you think you'll see her again?"

Floyd sighed. He picked up her card off the table and stared at it.

"I wish—" he said, and reached a decision. "No," he said finally, laying it face-down on the table.

"She likes you," Adams teased.

"I know," Floyd said. "And I'm flattered. But I don't need that kind of complication in my life right now. And it's not like I really care anyway."

He pushed his chair back and stood up, and though Adams knew he was lying, he said nothing.

Floyd walked away from the station, refusing to look back, but a part of him he couldn't silence kept wishing.

ƧNEⴷꓘ ꓒEEꓘ

Don't miss
Supervillain of the Day: Book 4
"Supervillain Hunters, International"
Coming June 4th, 2013!

Floyd hated mornings, especially when they were in the middle of the day. Especially when he'd overslept. Despite the fact that he'd accustomed himself to Earth's 24 hour daylight period he couldn't shake the feeling that a proper night's sleep was six hours, and anything longer than that left him disoriented and moody.

He was usually awake and at work by the time the sun came up in the morning, but by the time he sat up and wondered at what point in the previous day he'd been run over by a bulldozer it was after noon. That thought was so startling that it scared all the other thoughts out of his brain. It seemed particularly significant for some reason, but he couldn't remember any appointments he'd had.

It was a feeling that bothered him. He was also bothered by something else, something in connection with why he felt like he'd been run over by a bulldozer, but he told that something to shut up and go away until he figured out why he felt like there was somewhere he was supposed to be at noon on Thursday.

Thursday! He checked his watch and verified. It was indeed Thursday, and it was 12:55 local time. Grumbling in a language that wasn't English, and wasn't very polite either, he forced himself out of bed, into clean clothes and into the brilliantly lit outside world, not even bothering to try and force his door to close all the way. Outside traffic rumbled, horns honked, people talked, the wind was blowing, and it was quite clearly the middle of the day. Floyd took one look at it, and ran.

He ran past shoppers and students and business folk. He knocked down a small child, darted back to apologize, and then continued on his way. He elicited strange looks and the occasional insult, but he went too fast to hear them, and in ten minutes he was in a decidedly better mood. He almost ran past his destination, stopped abruptly, and heard the satisfying tinkle of a shop bell as he entered. He plopped into his usual seat, looked at Adams, and blinked.

Something was off.

"Good morning, officer," he said with genuine cheerfulness.

Adams didn't stir.

"I hope I haven't kept you waiting too long," Floyd pressed on, keeping his conscious mind occupied while his subconscious worked out what wasn't right. "I got detained last night, and overslept this morning and, you know how it goes. Alien planet and all."

He grinned at Adams, and waved the waitress over to give her his drink order. The only part of Adams that moved was his eyes, as he glanced first at Floyd, then at the waitress, and then back out the window to the busy street.

Floyd frowned.

"Is something wrong?" he asked abruptly.

Adams started, as though coming back to the real world. "No," he said abruptly. "Everything's fine."

"Oh." Floyd relaxed. His subconscious registered that as the first lie the police officer had ever told him, and kept on trying to figure things out.

"Thanks for getting me out of that jam last night," he continued. "I wasn't looking forward to the alternative."

Adams nodded absently, drifting back to wherever he'd been before Floyd had showed up.

Floyd frowned in concern. He drew his knees up to his chin, accepted the drink the waitress brought him, waved her off when she asked after their orders, and regarded Adams thoughtfully.

Something was definitely wrong.

"You're quiet today," he said finally. Adams didn't reply.

Floyd tried again.

"Am I in trouble?"

"No," Adams said shortly.

Floyd took over from his subconscious and began to analyze the situation. There were a lot of things bothering him today. He had almost forgotten to be here, he felt like he'd been run over by a bulldozer, and he hadn't properly sat down and remembered what had happened the previous day. He decided to start with that.

He'd been walking home from the offices of the London Star after a long argument with the Editor about the superhero trend. It was almost midnight. He'd been accosted by Two-face. They'd fought. Or rather, Two-face had fought and Floyd had tried to get away, and then Brawn had come along and thrown him through a department store window.

Well, that cleared up one thing, Floyd thought ruefully. A department store window would feel very similar to a bulldozer if one hit it the right way.

Then the police and the local villain conglomerate had had a showdown while he watched. He felt a twinge of guilt about the watching part, but decided to ignore it for the time being. He'd been held up by the police, and then Adams had come along and...

Floyd blinked.

"Something happened last night," he said abruptly.

"Nothing happened last night," Adams said too quickly.

"Yes, it did," Floyd argued. "You saved my hide, and then you sent me home. You never get me out of a scrape and send me home. You always keep me around to lecture and help clean up and so forth. And when I came in today you didn't say anything about me being late. You didn't say anything about last night. You didn't say anything at all. You've said two words since I walked in the door, and one was an outright lie. You never lie. Especially to me, because you're trying to be a good influence. So 'fess up and tell me; what is wrong?"

Adams smiled in spite of himself, but it was a sad, pathetic smile. He shifted in his seat and met Floyd's eyes briefly.

"I was suspended," he said simply.

To report a supervillain
or learn more about the series,
visit:

supervillainoftheday.com

A NOTE ABOUT ENGLAND

Being an American writing about England is one of the most terrifying and exhilarating things I have ever done. I've done my best to be as accurate as possible when setting this series in London, but we're all human and can make mistakes. If you're an expert or a resident of England and you find an error in this narrative, be sure to let me know about it! I'll take the correction under consideration when writing future novels, and possibly even correct the error in the omnibus version.

Submit errors using the form provided on supervillainoftheday.com and you could earn yourself a copy of the ebook version of the next novel in the series!

ABOUT THE AUTHOR

Katie is a writer of many talents, constantly branching out into new fields and genres. She primarily writes novels and short stories in the science fiction and fantasy genres, along with an assortment of hilarious and sentimental poetry. When she's not writing she's acting, directing, singing, playing her Celtic harp or songwriting, often engaging in more than one at a time. She lives in the beautiful hills of Kentucky with her parents and eight siblings.

Visit her website at katielynndaniels.com

Or follow her on twitter @danielskatie